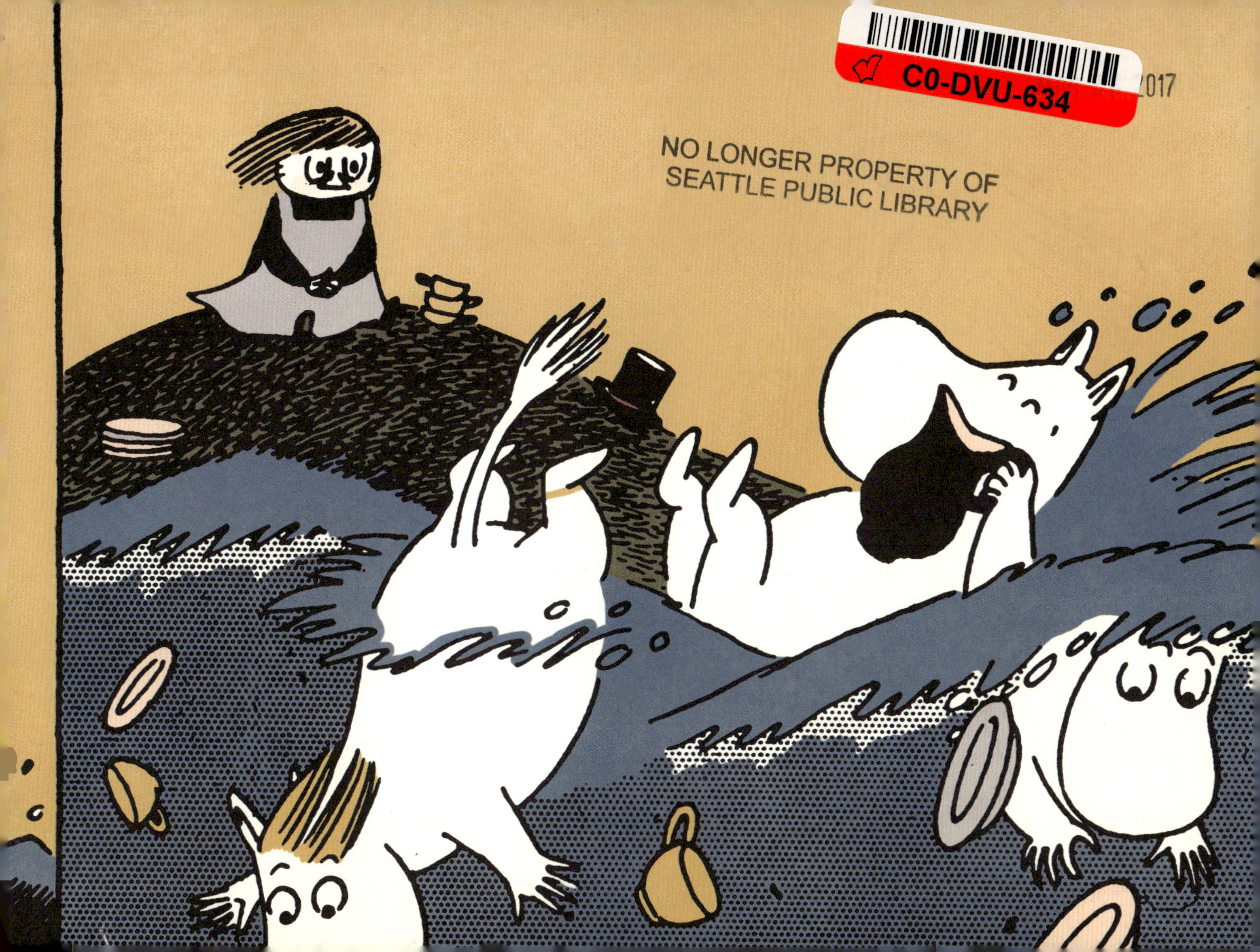

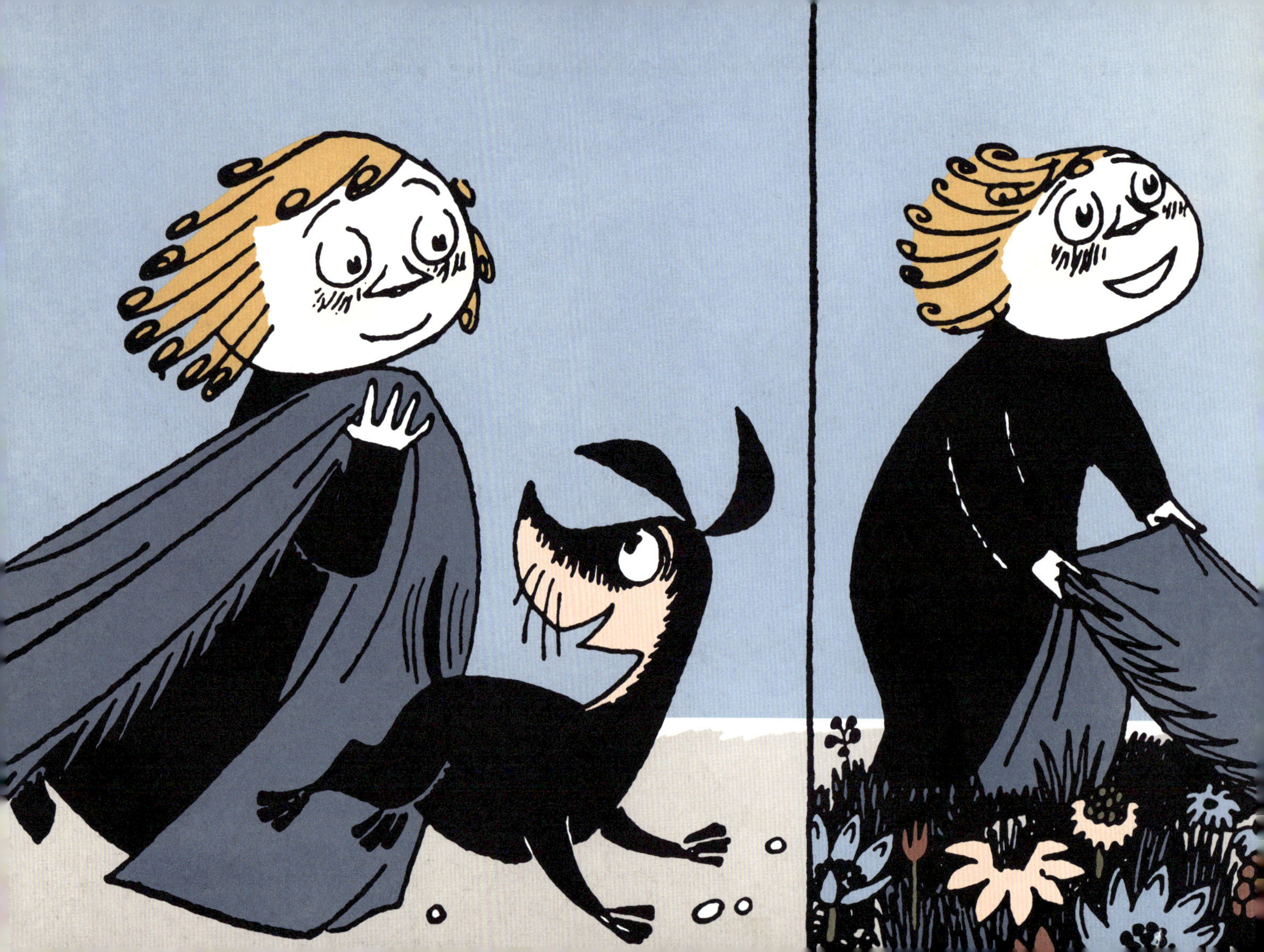

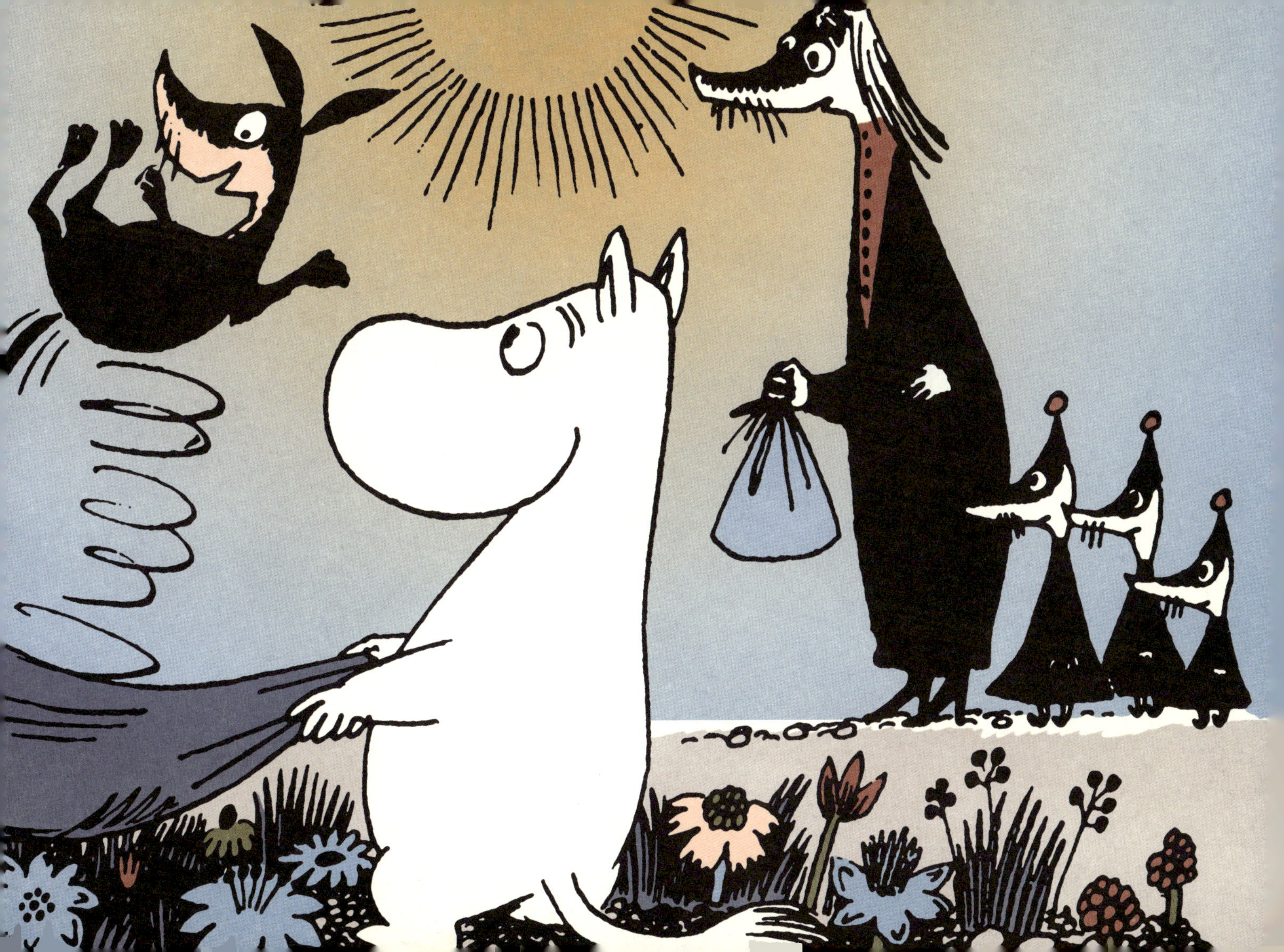

Enfant is an imprint of Drawn & Quarterly.

drawnandquarterly.com

First edition: September 2015
Printed in Malaysia
10 9 8 7 6 5 4 3 2 1

Library and Archives Canada Cataloguing in Publication
Jansson, Tove, author, illustrator
Moominmamma's Maid / Tove Jansson.
A selection from the Moomin comic strip series originally published
in the British newspaper, the *Evening News* (1956).
ISBN 978-1-77046-216-8 (pbk.)
I. Jansson, Tove. Moomin. 1I. Comic books, strips, etc. III. Title.
PZ7.7.J35Moma 2015 j741.5'94897 C2015-902371-8

Published in the USA by Enfant, a client
publisher of Farrar, Straus and Giroux
Orders: 888.330.8477

Published in Canada by Enfant, a client
publisher of Raincoast Books
Orders: 800.663.5714

Distributed in the United Kingdom
by Publishers Group UK
Orders: info@pguk.co.uk

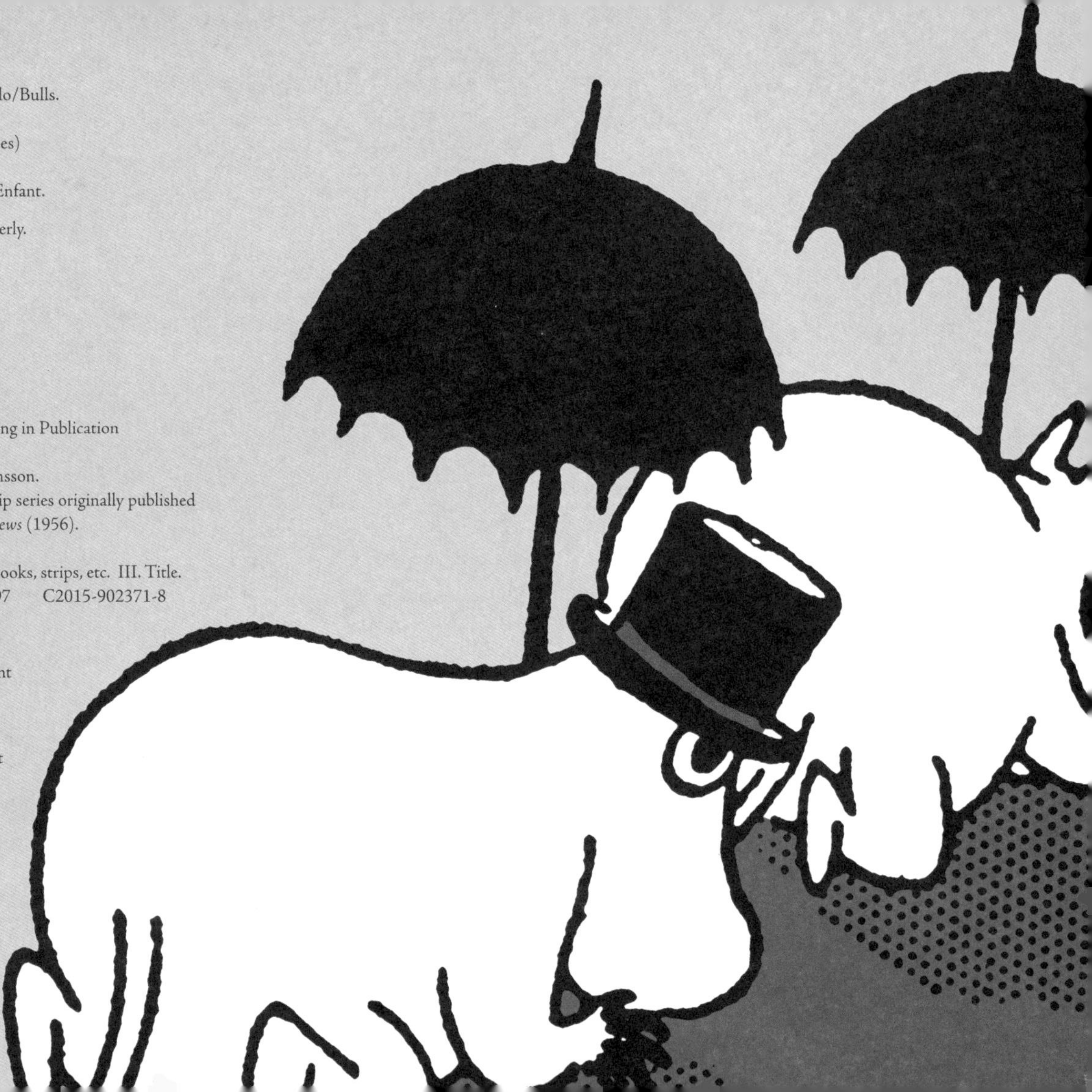

MOOMINMAMMA'S MAID *Tove Jansson*

ENFANT

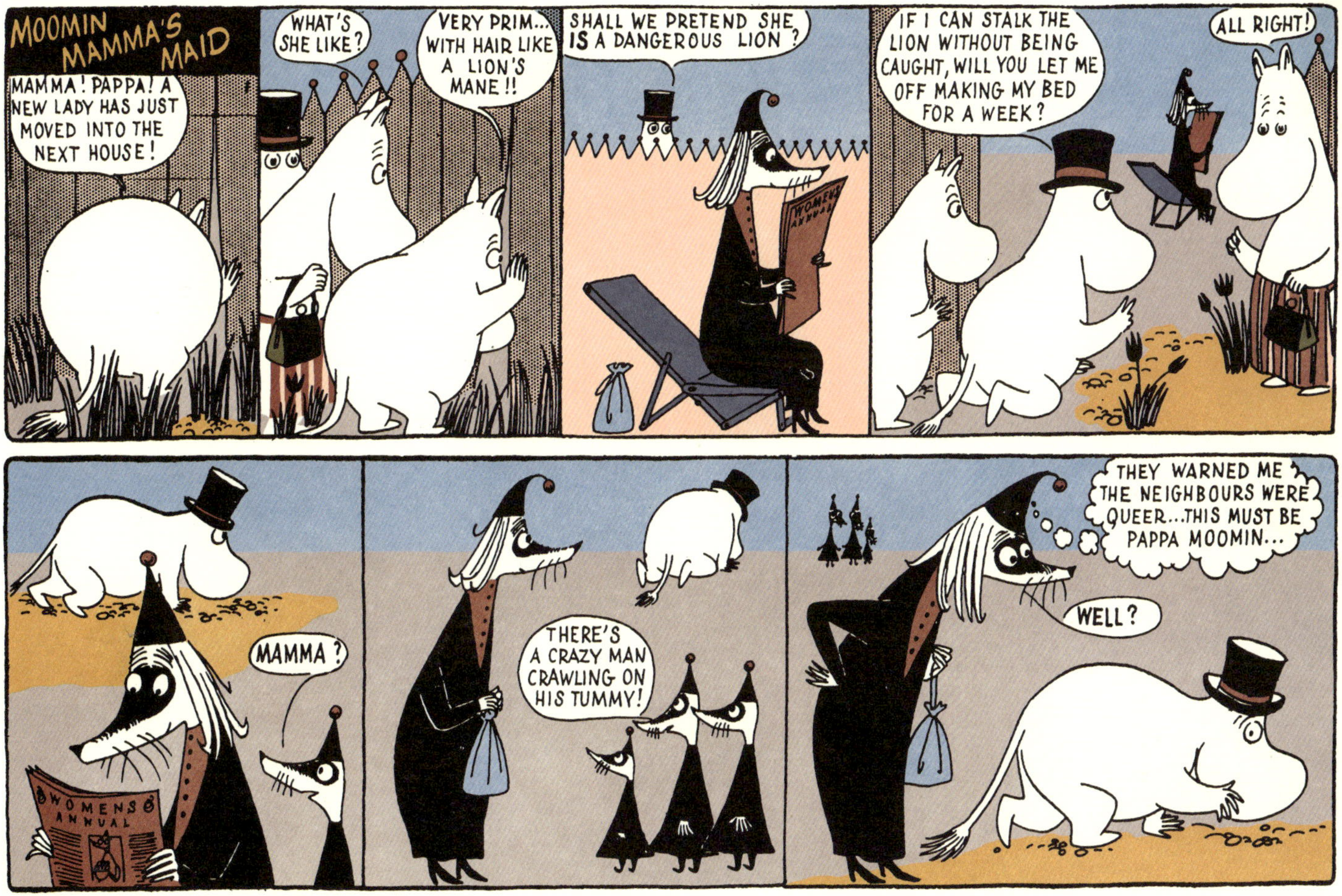
MOOMIN MAMMA'S MAID
MAMMA! PAPPA! A NEW LADY HAS JUST MOVED INTO THE NEXT HOUSE!
WHAT'S SHE LIKE?
VERY PRIM... WITH HAIR LIKE A LION'S MANE!!
SHALL WE PRETEND SHE **IS** A DANGEROUS LION?
WOMENS ANNUAL
IF I CAN STALK THE LION WITHOUT BEING CAUGHT, WILL YOU LET ME OFF MAKING MY BED FOR A WEEK?
ALL RIGHT!
MAMMA?
WOMENS ANNUAL
THERE'S A CRAZY MAN CRAWLING ON HIS TUMMY!
THEY WARNED ME THE NEIGHBOURS WERE QUEER...THIS MUST BE PAPPA MOOMIN...
WELL?

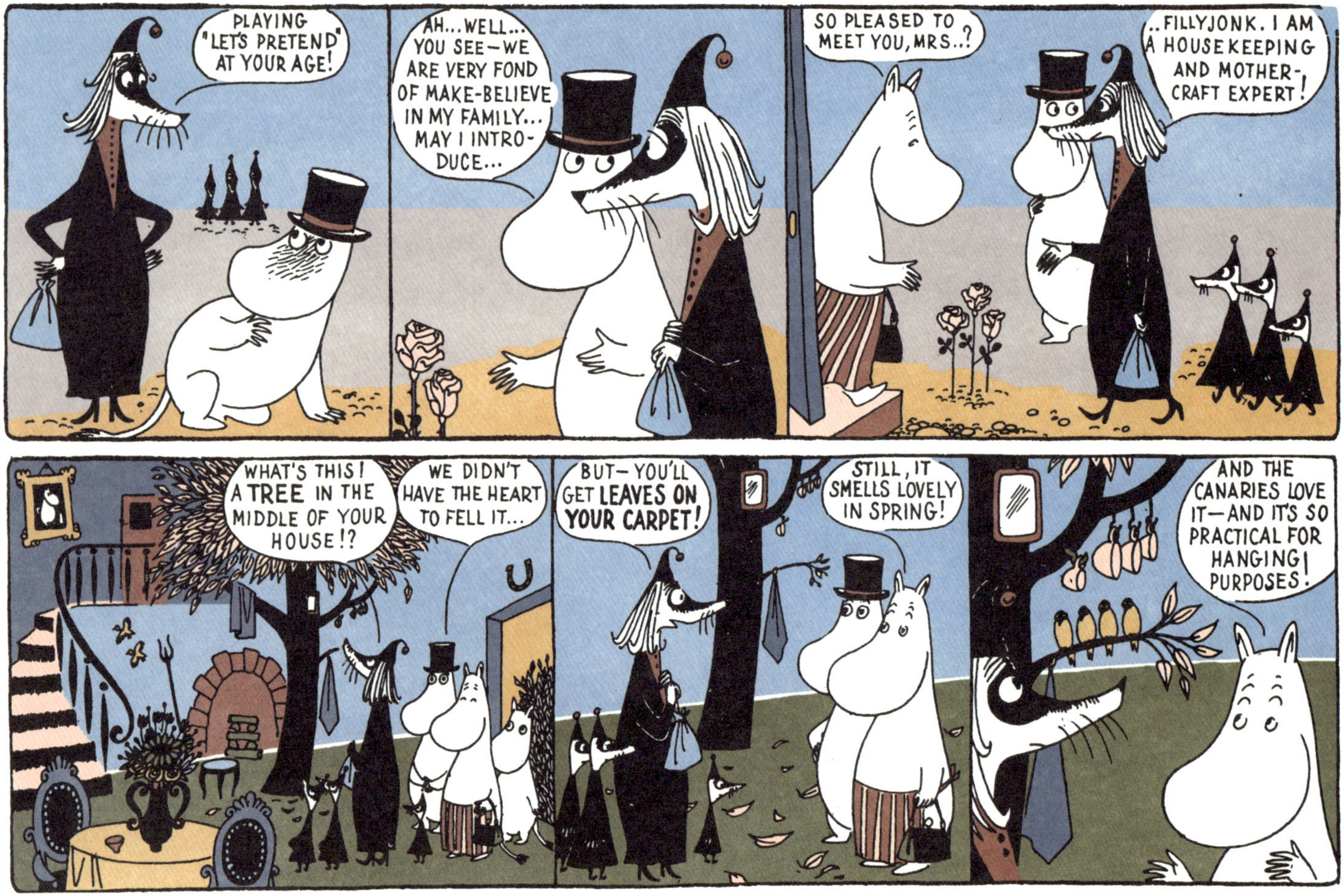
PLAYING "LET'S PRETEND" AT YOUR AGE!
AH... WELL... YOU SEE—WE ARE VERY FOND OF MAKE-BELIEVE IN MY FAMILY... MAY I INTRODUCE...
SO PLEASED TO MEET YOU, MRS..?
..FILLYJONK. I AM A HOUSEKEEPING AND MOTHER-CRAFT EXPERT!
WHAT'S THIS! A TREE IN THE MIDDLE OF YOUR HOUSE!?
WE DIDN'T HAVE THE HEART TO FELL IT...
BUT—YOU'LL GET LEAVES ON YOUR CARPET!
STILL, IT SMELLS LOVELY IN SPRING!
AND THE CANARIES LOVE IT—AND IT'S SO PRACTICAL FOR HANGING PURPOSES!

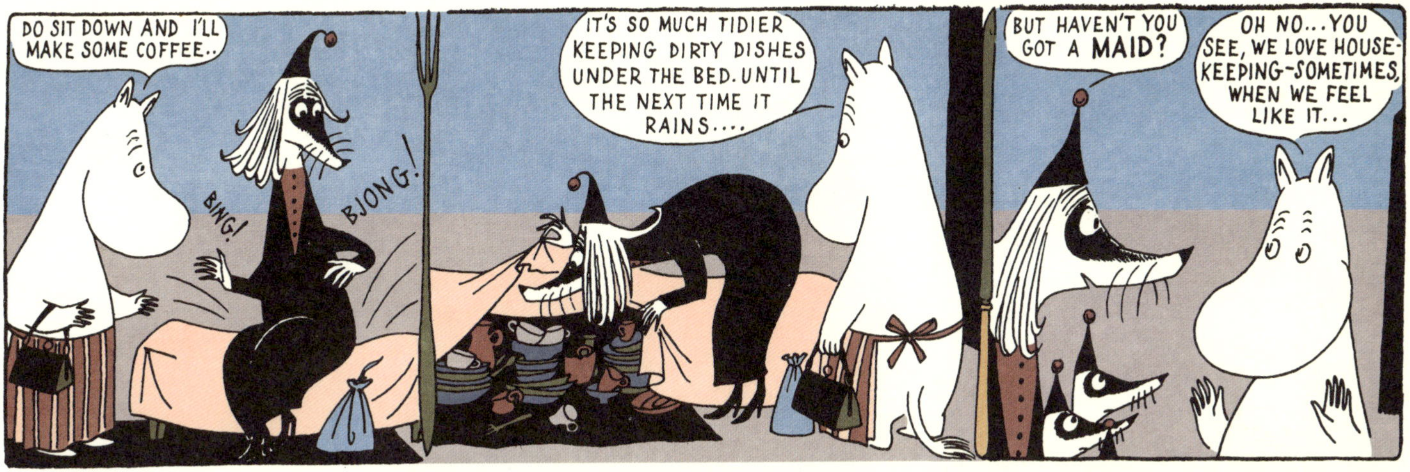
DO SIT DOWN AND I'LL MAKE SOME COFFEE..
BING!
BJONG!
IT'S SO MUCH TIDIER KEEPING DIRTY DISHES UNDER THE BED. UNTIL THE NEXT TIME IT RAINS....
BUT HAVEN'T YOU GOT A MAID?
OH NO...YOU SEE, WE LOVE HOUSE-KEEPING-SOMETIMES, WHEN WE FEEL LIKE IT...

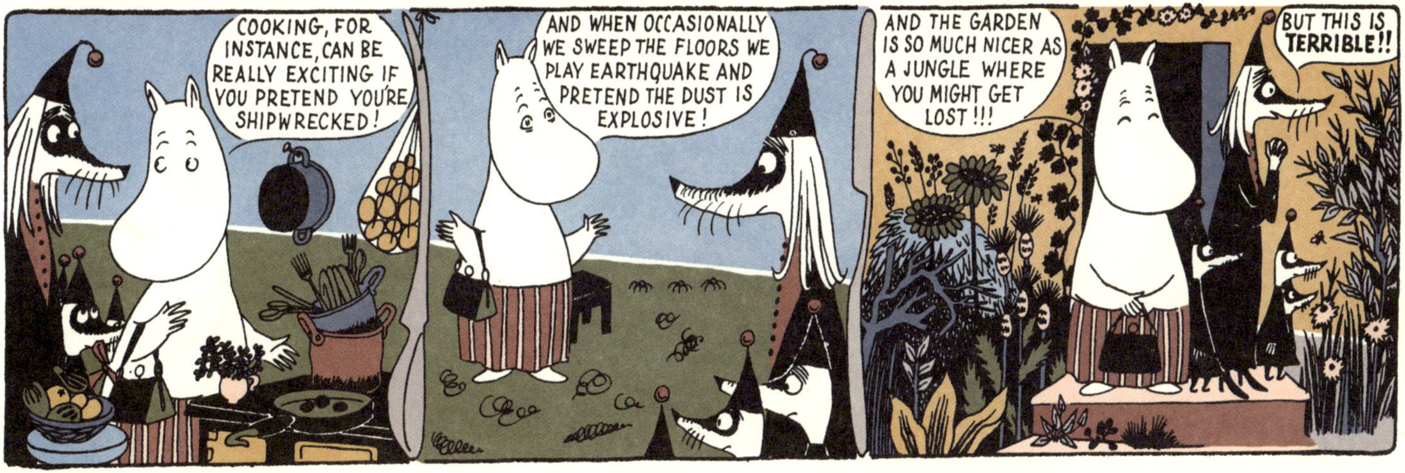
COOKING, FOR INSTANCE, CAN BE REALLY EXCITING IF YOU PRETEND YOU'RE SHIPWRECKED!
AND WHEN OCCASIONALLY WE SWEEP THE FLOORS WE PLAY EARTHQUAKE AND PRETEND THE DUST IS EXPLOSIVE!
AND THE GARDEN IS SO MUCH NICER AS A JUNGLE WHERE YOU MIGHT GET LOST!!!
BUT THIS IS TERRIBLE!!

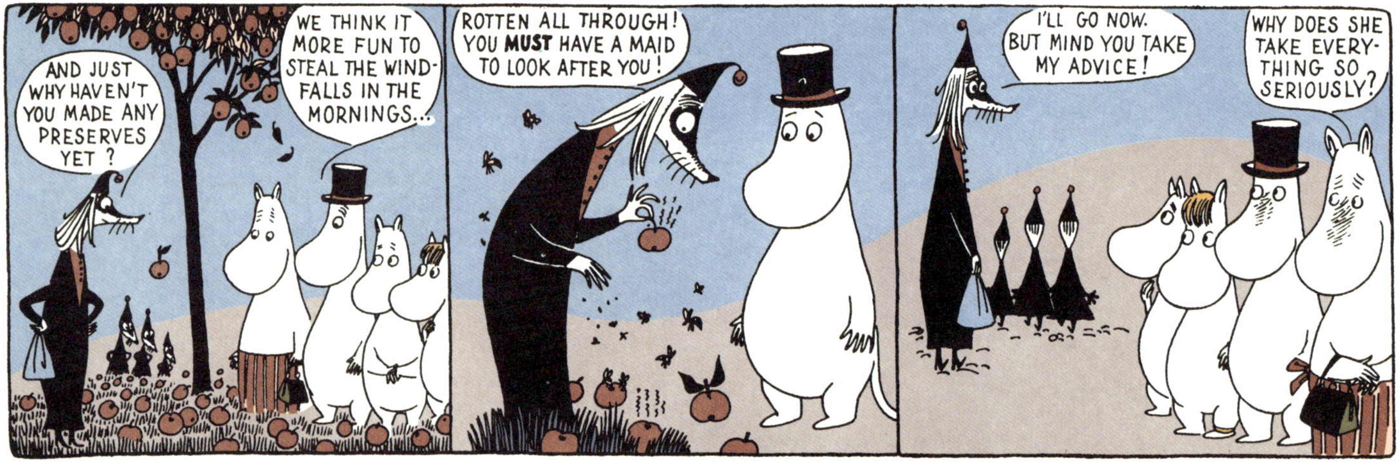
AND JUST WHY HAVEN'T YOU MADE ANY PRESERVES YET ?
WE THINK IT MORE FUN TO STEAL THE WIND-FALLS IN THE MORNINGS...
ROTTEN ALL THROUGH! YOU **MUST** HAVE A MAID TO LOOK AFTER YOU !
I'LL GO NOW. BUT MIND YOU TAKE MY ADVICE !
WHY DOES SHE TAKE EVERY-THING SO SERIOUSLY?

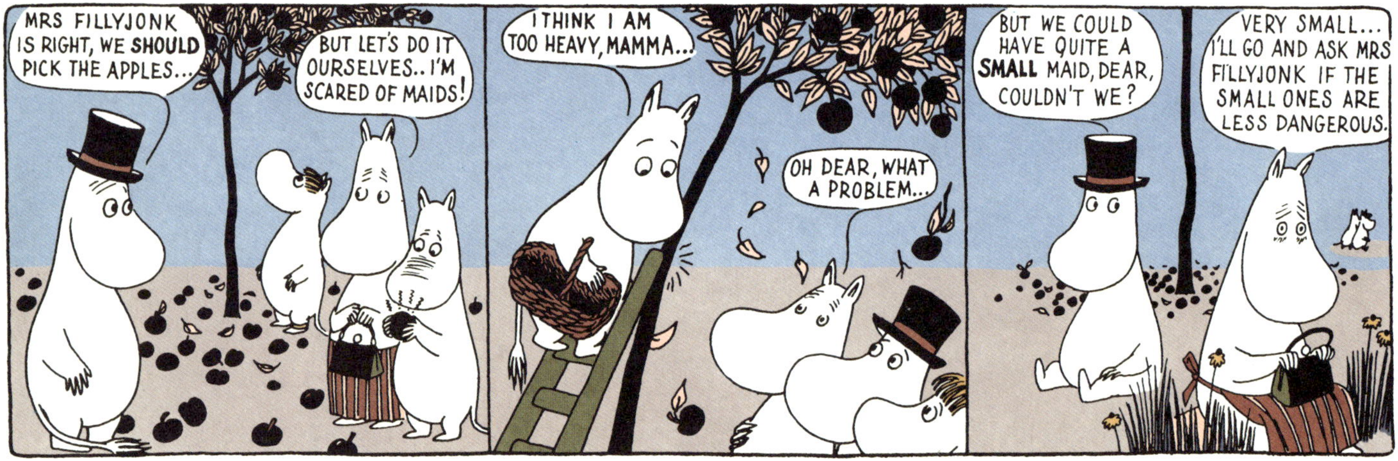
MRS FILLYJONK IS RIGHT, WE **SHOULD** PICK THE APPLES...
BUT LET'S DO IT OURSELVES.. I'M SCARED OF MAIDS!
I THINK I AM TOO HEAVY, MAMMA...
OH DEAR, WHAT A PROBLEM...
BUT WE COULD HAVE QUITE A **SMALL** MAID, DEAR, COULDN'T WE ?
VERY SMALL... I'LL GO AND ASK MRS FILLYJONK IF THE SMALL ONES ARE LESS DANGEROUS.

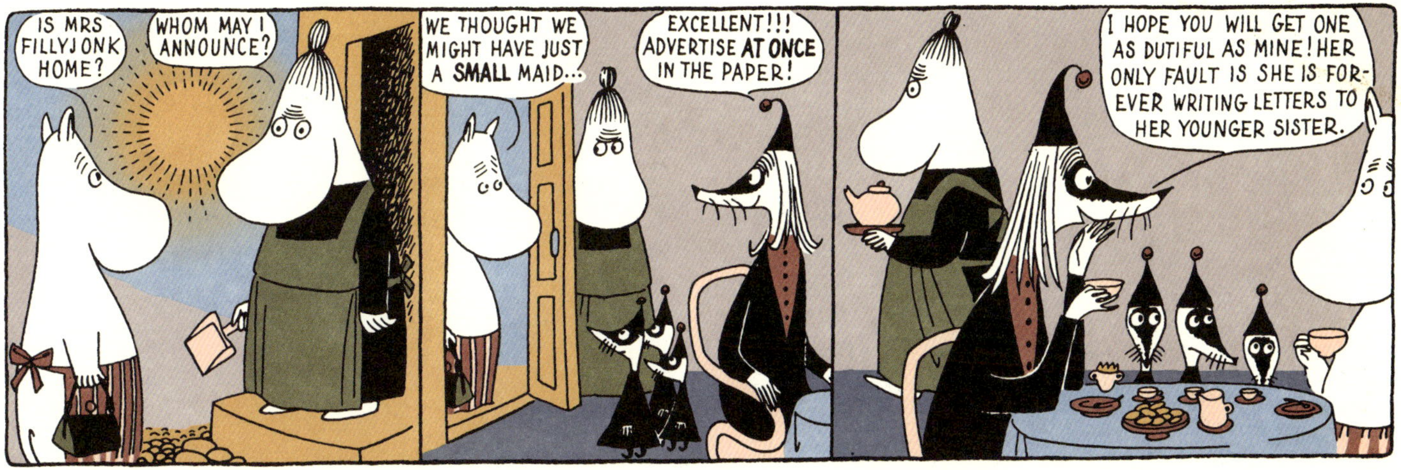
IS MRS FILLYJONK HOME?
WHOM MAY I ANNOUNCE?
WE THOUGHT WE MIGHT HAVE JUST A **SMALL** MAID...
EXCELLENT!!! ADVERTISE **AT ONCE** IN THE PAPER!
I HOPE YOU WILL GET ONE AS DUTIFUL AS MINE! HER ONLY FAULT IS SHE IS FOR-EVER WRITING LETTERS TO HER YOUNGER SISTER.

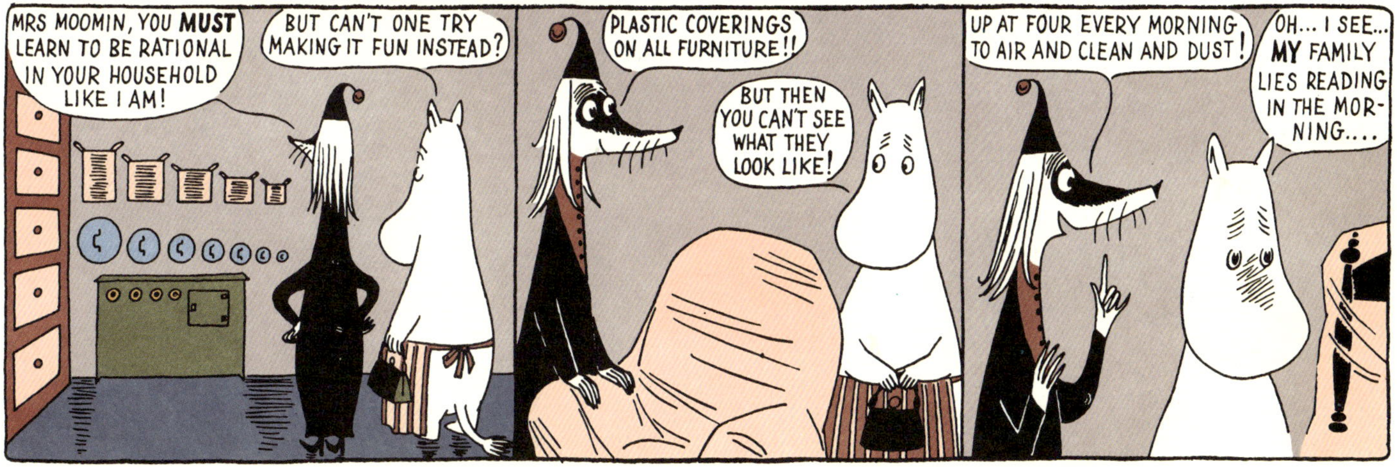
MRS MOOMIN, YOU **MUST** LEARN TO BE RATIONAL IN YOUR HOUSEHOLD LIKE I AM!
BUT CAN'T ONE TRY MAKING IT FUN INSTEAD?
PLASTIC COVERINGS ON ALL FURNITURE!!
BUT THEN YOU CAN'T SEE WHAT THEY LOOK LIKE!
UP AT FOUR EVERY MORNING TO AIR AND CLEAN AND DUST!
OH... I SEE... **MY** FAMILY LIES READING IN THE MOR-NING....

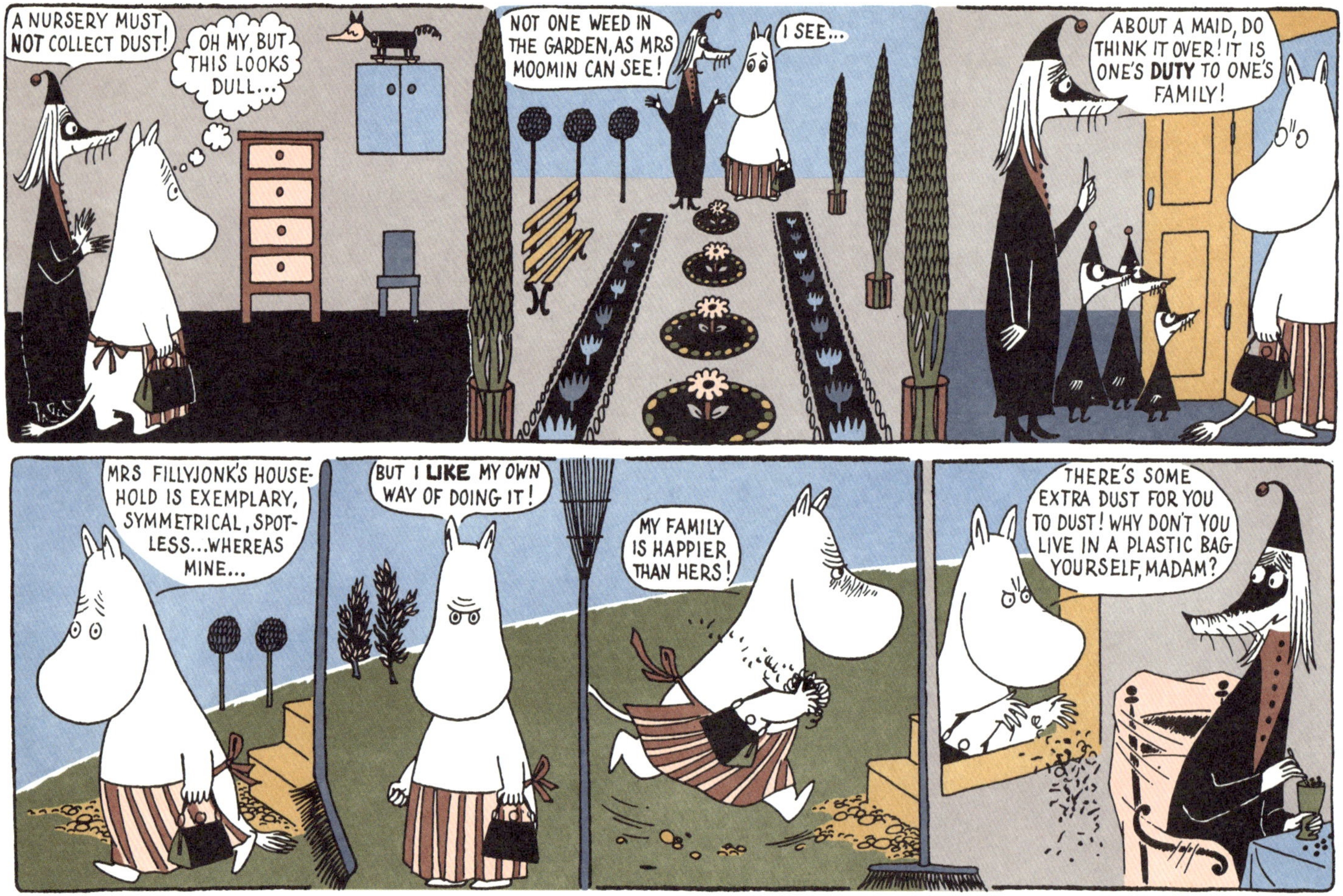
A NURSERY MUST **NOT** COLLECT DUST!
OH MY, BUT THIS LOOKS DULL...
NOT ONE WEED IN THE GARDEN, AS MRS MOOMIN CAN SEE!
I SEE...
ABOUT A MAID, DO THINK IT OVER! IT IS ONE'S **DUTY** TO ONE'S FAMILY!
MRS FILLYJONK'S HOUSEHOLD IS EXEMPLARY, SYMMETRICAL, SPOTLESS...WHEREAS MINE...
BUT I **LIKE** MY OWN WAY OF DOING IT!
MY FAMILY IS HAPPIER THAN HERS!
THERE'S SOME EXTRA DUST FOR YOU TO DUST! WHY DON'T YOU LIVE IN A PLASTIC BAG YOURSELF, MADAM?

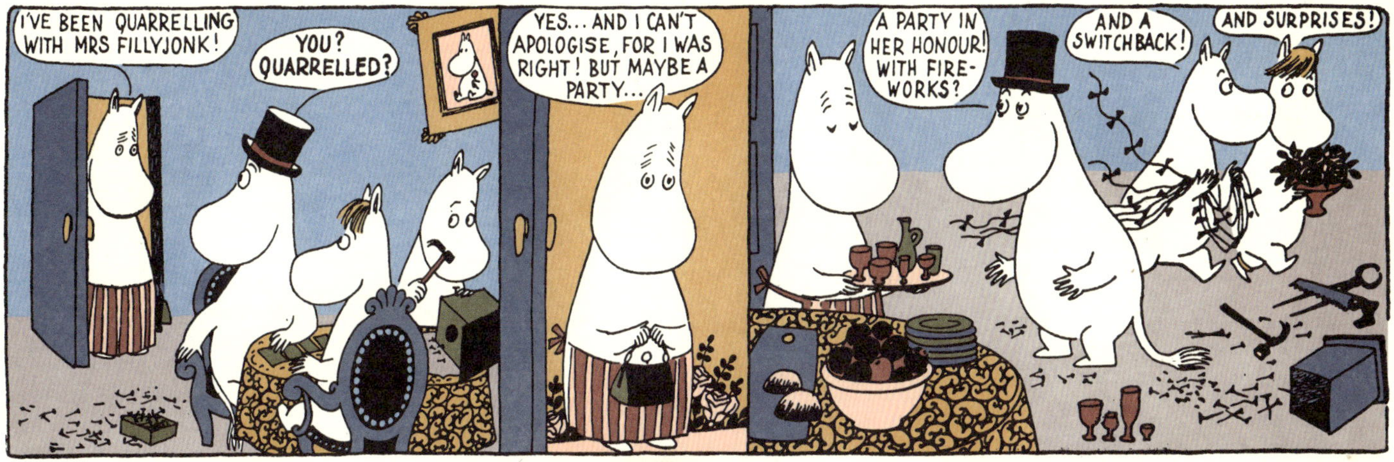
I'VE BEEN QUARRELLING WITH MRS FILLYJONK!
YOU? QUARRELLED?
YES... AND I CAN'T APOLOGISE, FOR I WAS RIGHT! BUT MAYBE A PARTY...
A PARTY IN HER HONOUR! WITH FIRE-WORKS?
AND A SWITCHBACK!
AND SURPRISES!

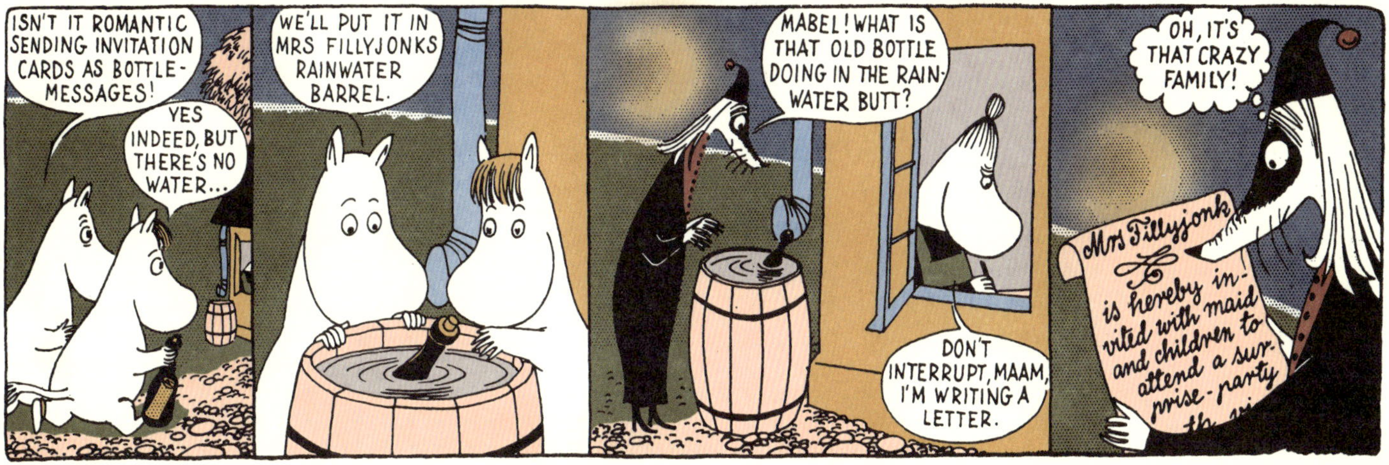
ISN'T IT ROMANTIC SENDING INVITATION CARDS AS BOTTLE-MESSAGES!
YES INDEED, BUT THERE'S NO WATER...
WE'LL PUT IT IN MRS FILLYJONKS RAINWATER BARREL.
MABEL! WHAT IS THAT OLD BOTTLE DOING IN THE RAIN-WATER BUTT?
DON'T INTERRUPT, MAAM, I'M WRITING A LETTER.
OH, IT'S THAT CRAZY FAMILY!
Mrs Fillyjonk
is hereby in-
vited with maid
and children to
attend a sur-
prise-party

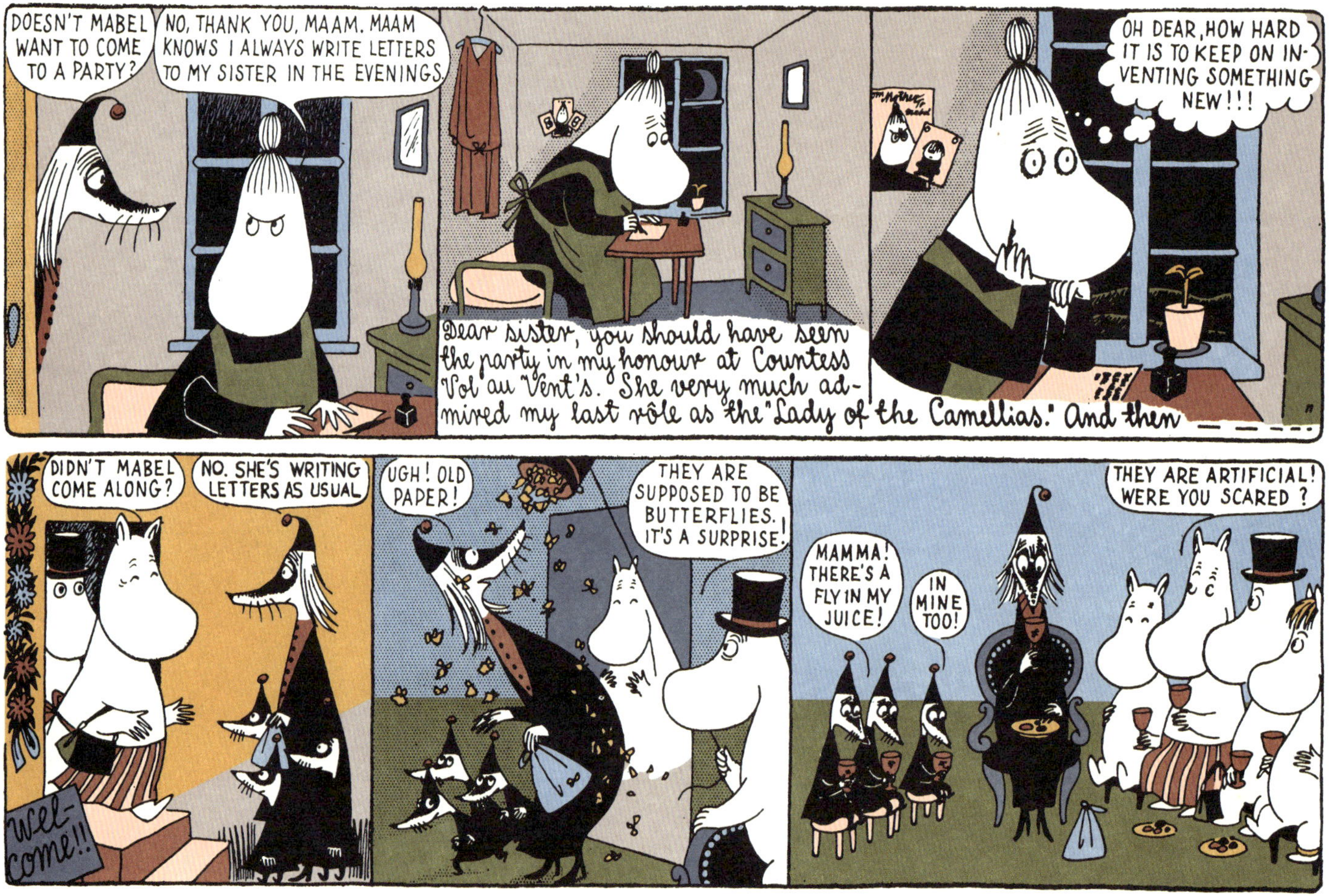
DOESN'T MABEL WANT TO COME TO A PARTY?
NO, THANK YOU, MAAM. MAAM KNOWS I ALWAYS WRITE LETTERS TO MY SISTER IN THE EVENINGS.
Dear sister, you should have seen the party in my honour at Countess Vol au Vent's. She very much admired my last rôle as the "Lady of the Camellias." And then
OH DEAR, HOW HARD IT IS TO KEEP ON INVENTING SOMETHING NEW!!!
DIDN'T MABEL COME ALONG?
NO. SHE'S WRITING LETTERS AS USUAL
WEL-COME!!
UGH! OLD PAPER!
THEY ARE SUPPOSED TO BE BUTTERFLIES. IT'S A SURPRISE!
MAMMA! THERE'S A FLY IN MY JUICE!
IN MINE TOO!
THEY ARE ARTIFICIAL! WERE YOU SCARED?

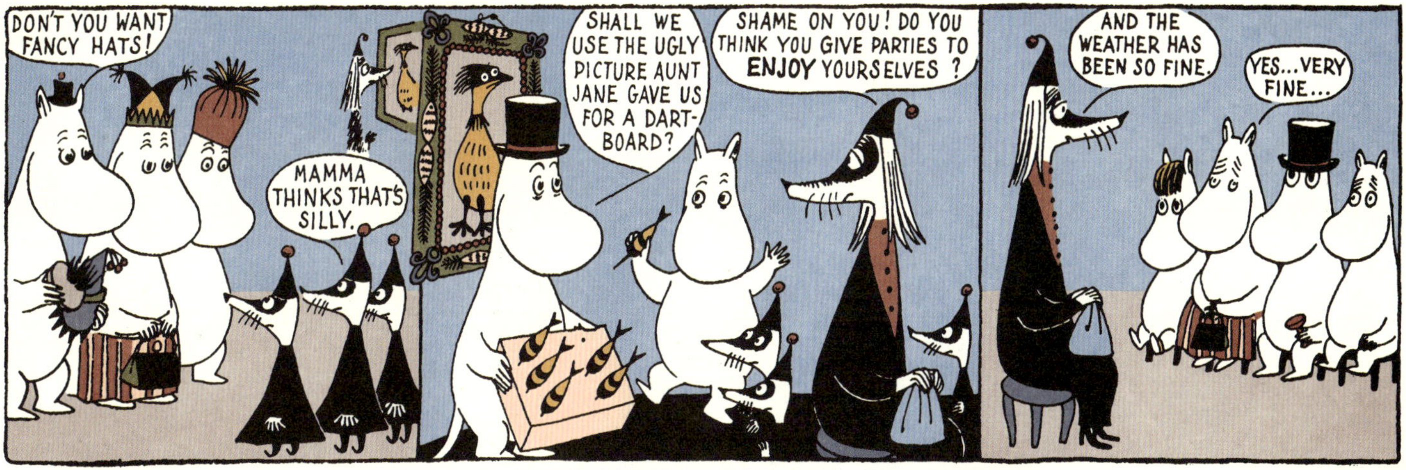
DON'T YOU WANT FANCY HATS!
MAMMA THINKS THAT'S SILLY.
SHALL WE USE THE UGLY PICTURE AUNT JANE GAVE US FOR A DART-BOARD?
SHAME ON YOU! DO YOU THINK YOU GIVE PARTIES TO ENJOY YOURSELVES ?
AND THE WEATHER HAS BEEN SO FINE.
YES... VERY FINE...

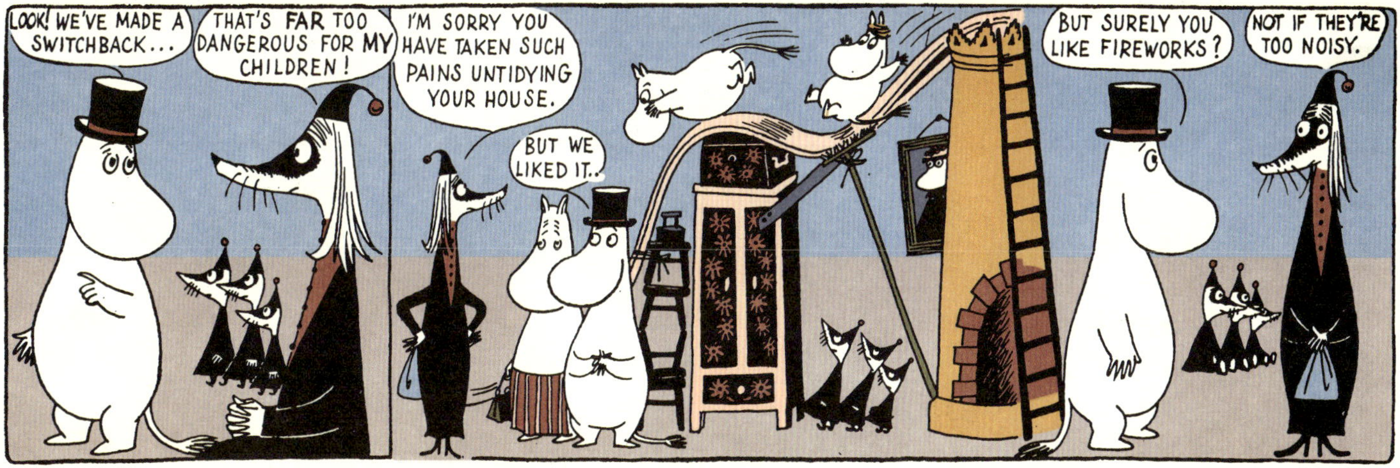
LOOK! WE'VE MADE A SWITCHBACK...
THAT'S FAR TOO DANGEROUS FOR MY CHILDREN!
I'M SORRY YOU HAVE TAKEN SUCH PAINS UNTIDYING YOUR HOUSE.
BUT WE LIKED IT..
BUT SURELY YOU LIKE FIREWORKS?
NOT IF THEY'RE TOO NOISY.

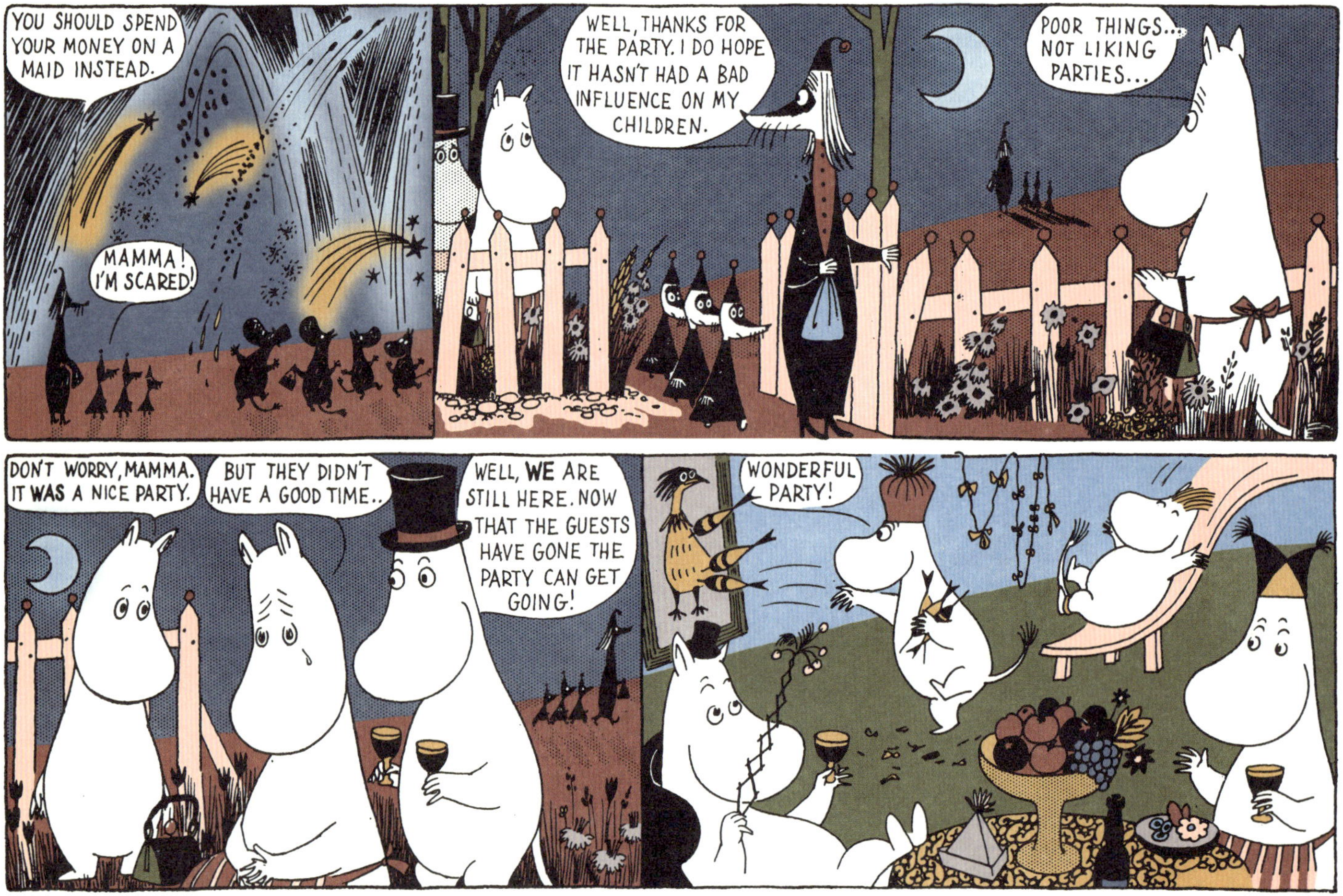
YOU SHOULD SPEND YOUR MONEY ON A MAID INSTEAD.
MAMMA! I'M SCARED!
WELL, THANKS FOR THE PARTY. I DO HOPE IT HASN'T HAD A BAD INFLUENCE ON MY CHILDREN.
POOR THINGS... NOT LIKING PARTIES...
DON'T WORRY, MAMMA. IT WAS A NICE PARTY.
BUT THEY DIDN'T HAVE A GOOD TIME..
WELL, WE ARE STILL HERE. NOW THAT THE GUESTS HAVE GONE THE PARTY CAN GET GOING!
WONDERFUL PARTY!

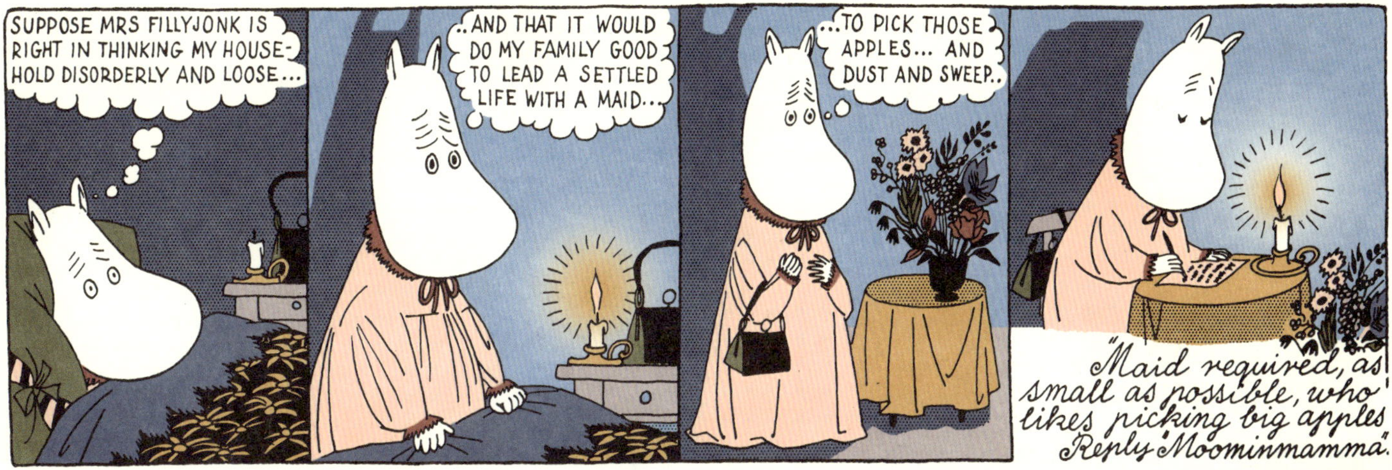
SUPPOSE MRS FILLYJONK IS RIGHT IN THINKING MY HOUSE-HOLD DISORDERLY AND LOOSE...
..AND THAT IT WOULD DO MY FAMILY GOOD TO LEAD A SETTLED LIFE WITH A MAID...
...TO PICK THOSE APPLES... AND DUST AND SWEEP..
"Maid required, as small as possible, who likes picking big apples Reply 'Moominmamma'.

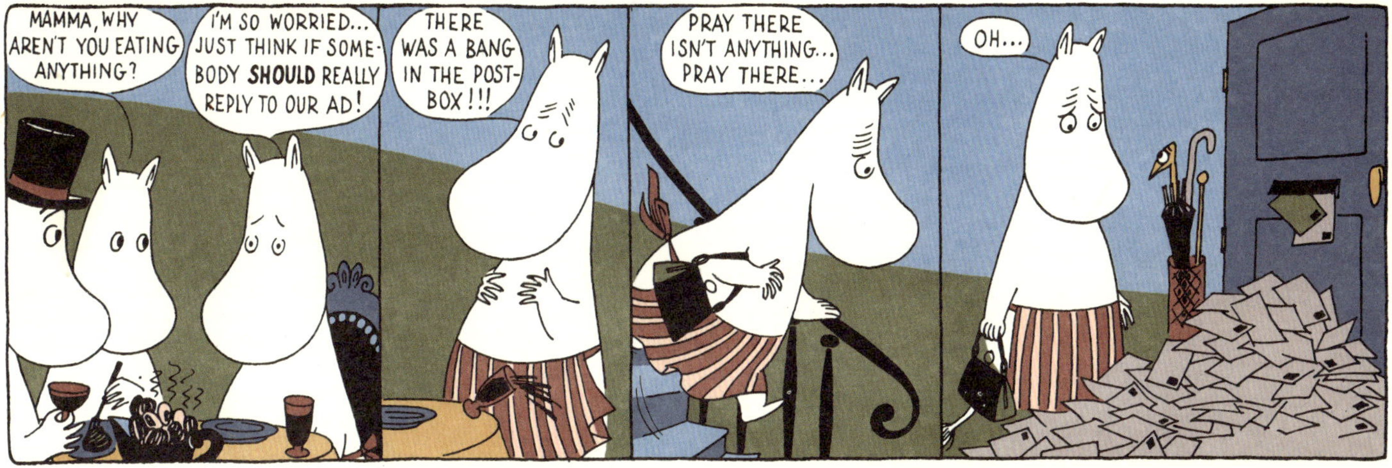
MAMMA, WHY AREN'T YOU EATING ANYTHING?
I'M SO WORRIED... JUST THINK IF SOME-BODY SHOULD REALLY REPLY TO OUR AD!
THERE WAS A BANG IN THE POST-BOX!!!
PRAY THERE ISN'T ANYTHING... PRAY THERE...
OH...

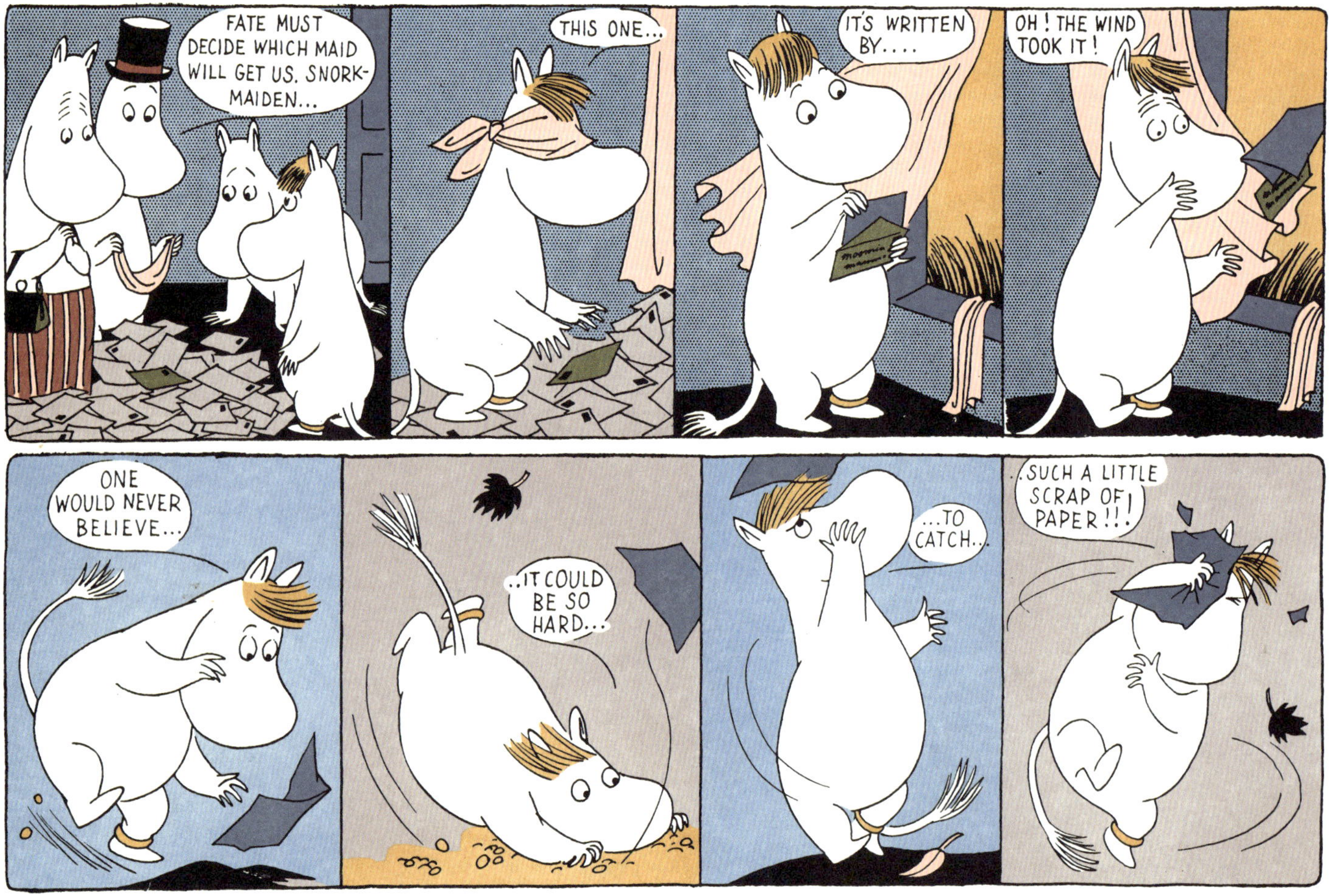
FATE MUST DECIDE WHICH MAID WILL GET US. SNORK-MAIDEN...
THIS ONE...
IT'S WRITTEN BY....
OH! THE WIND TOOK IT!
ONE WOULD NEVER BELIEVE...
..IT COULD BE SO HARD...
...TO CATCH...
..SUCH A LITTLE SCRAP OF PAPER!!!

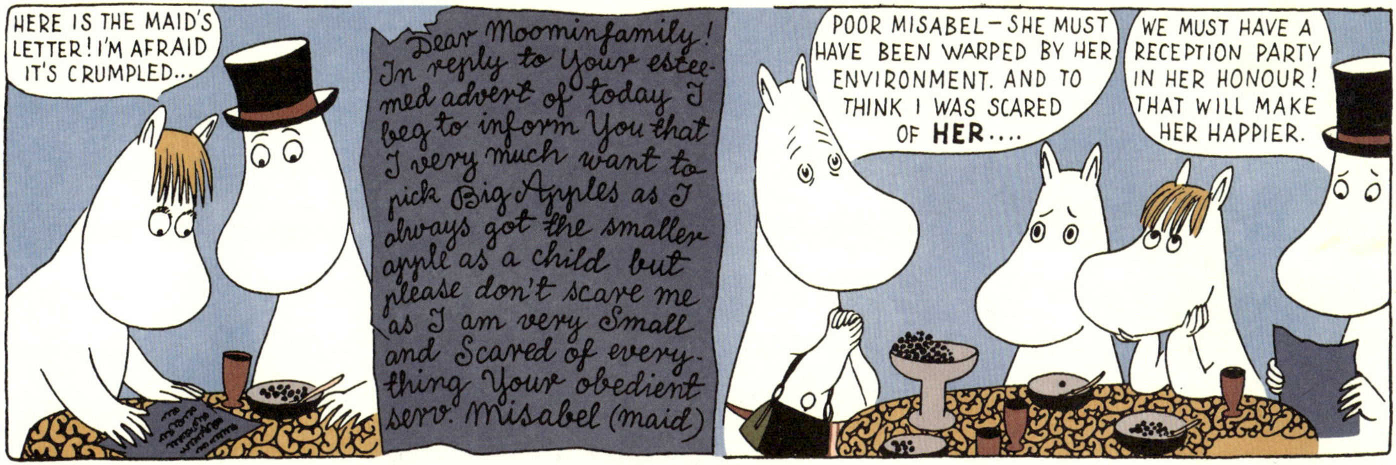
HERE IS THE MAID'S LETTER! I'M AFRAID IT'S CRUMPLED...
Dear Moominfamily! In reply to Your esteemed advert of today I beg to inform You that I very much want to pick Big Apples as I always got the smaller apple as a child but please don't scare me as I am very Small and Scared of everything Your obedient serv. Misabel (maid)
POOR MISABEL – SHE MUST HAVE BEEN WARPED BY HER ENVIRONMENT. AND TO THINK I WAS SCARED OF **HER**....
WE MUST HAVE A RECEPTION PARTY IN HER HONOUR! THAT WILL MAKE HER HAPPIER.

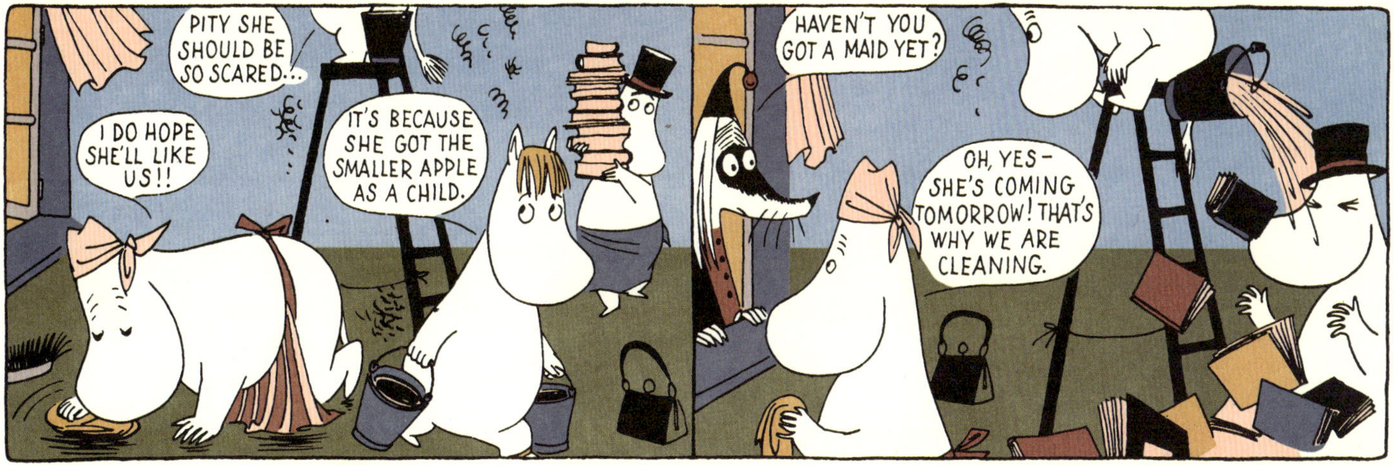
PITY SHE SHOULD BE SO SCARED...
I DO HOPE SHE'LL LIKE US!!
IT'S BECAUSE SHE GOT THE SMALLER APPLE AS A CHILD.
HAVEN'T YOU GOT A MAID YET?
OH, YES – SHE'S COMING TOMORROW! THAT'S WHY WE ARE CLEANING.

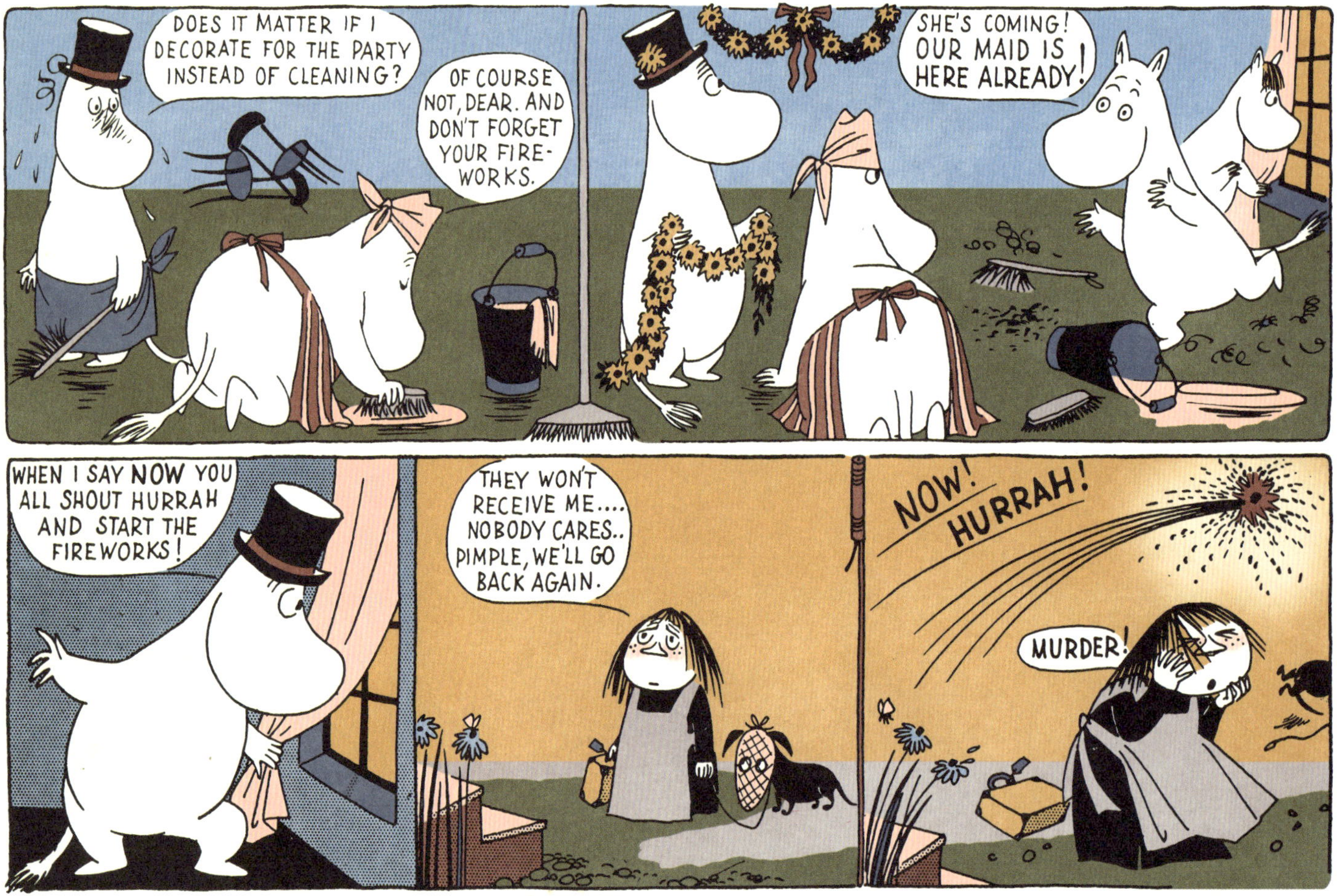
DOES IT MATTER IF I DECORATE FOR THE PARTY INSTEAD OF CLEANING?
OF COURSE NOT, DEAR. AND DON'T FORGET YOUR FIRE-WORKS.
SHE'S COMING! OUR MAID IS HERE ALREADY!
WHEN I SAY NOW YOU ALL SHOUT HURRAH AND START THE FIREWORKS!
THEY WON'T RECEIVE ME.... NOBODY CARES.. PIMPLE, WE'LL GO BACK AGAIN.
NOW!
HURRAH!
MURDER!

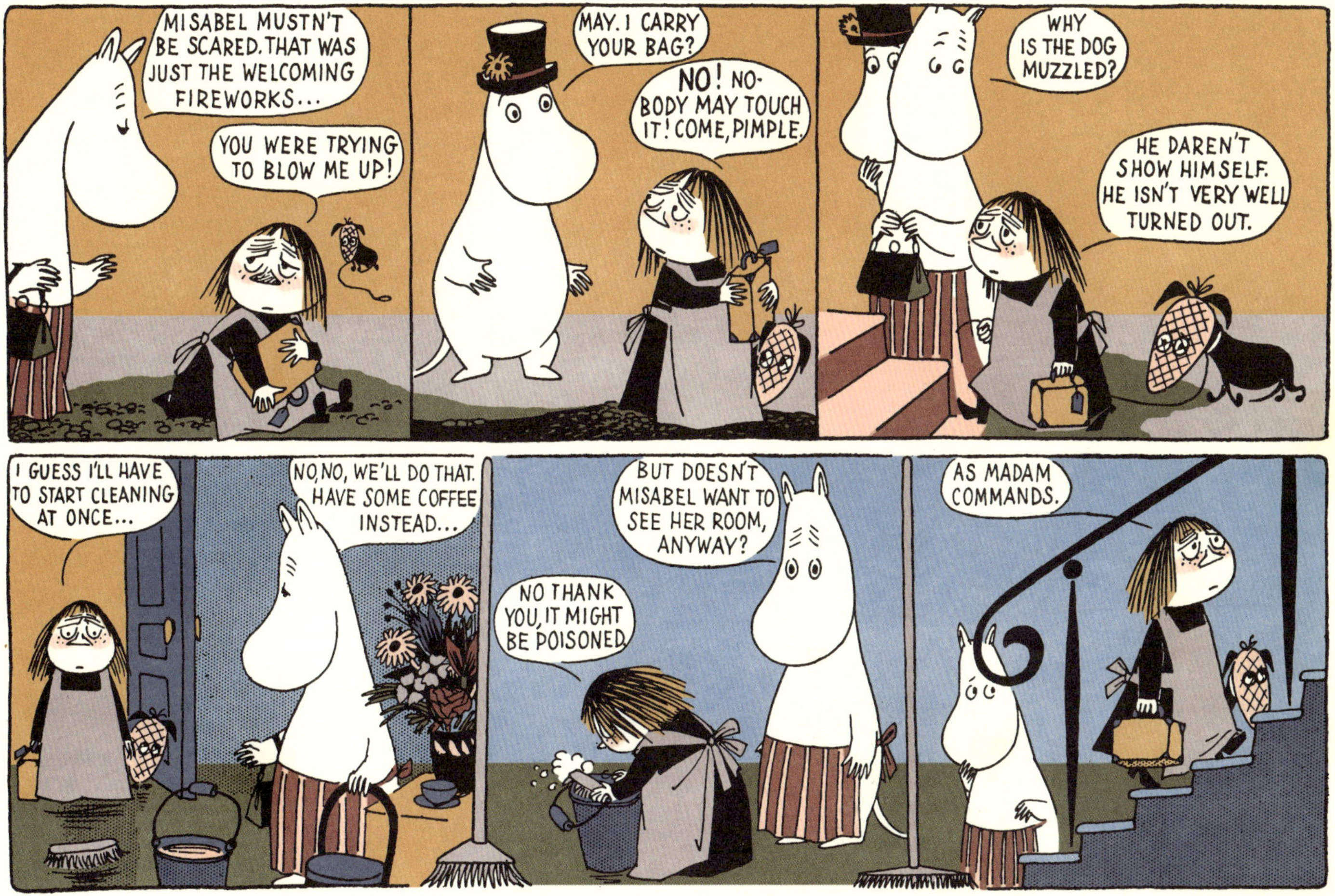
MISABEL MUSTN'T BE SCARED. THAT WAS JUST THE WELCOMING FIREWORKS...
YOU WERE TRYING TO BLOW ME UP!
MAY. I CARRY YOUR BAG?
NO! NOBODY MAY TOUCH IT! COME, PIMPLE.
WHY IS THE DOG MUZZLED?
HE DAREN'T SHOW HIMSELF. HE ISN'T VERY WELL TURNED OUT.
I GUESS I'LL HAVE TO START CLEANING AT ONCE...
NO, NO, WE'LL DO THAT. HAVE SOME COFFEE INSTEAD...
BUT DOESN'T MISABEL WANT TO SEE HER ROOM, ANYWAY?
NO THANK YOU, IT MIGHT BE POISONED.
AS MADAM COMMANDS.

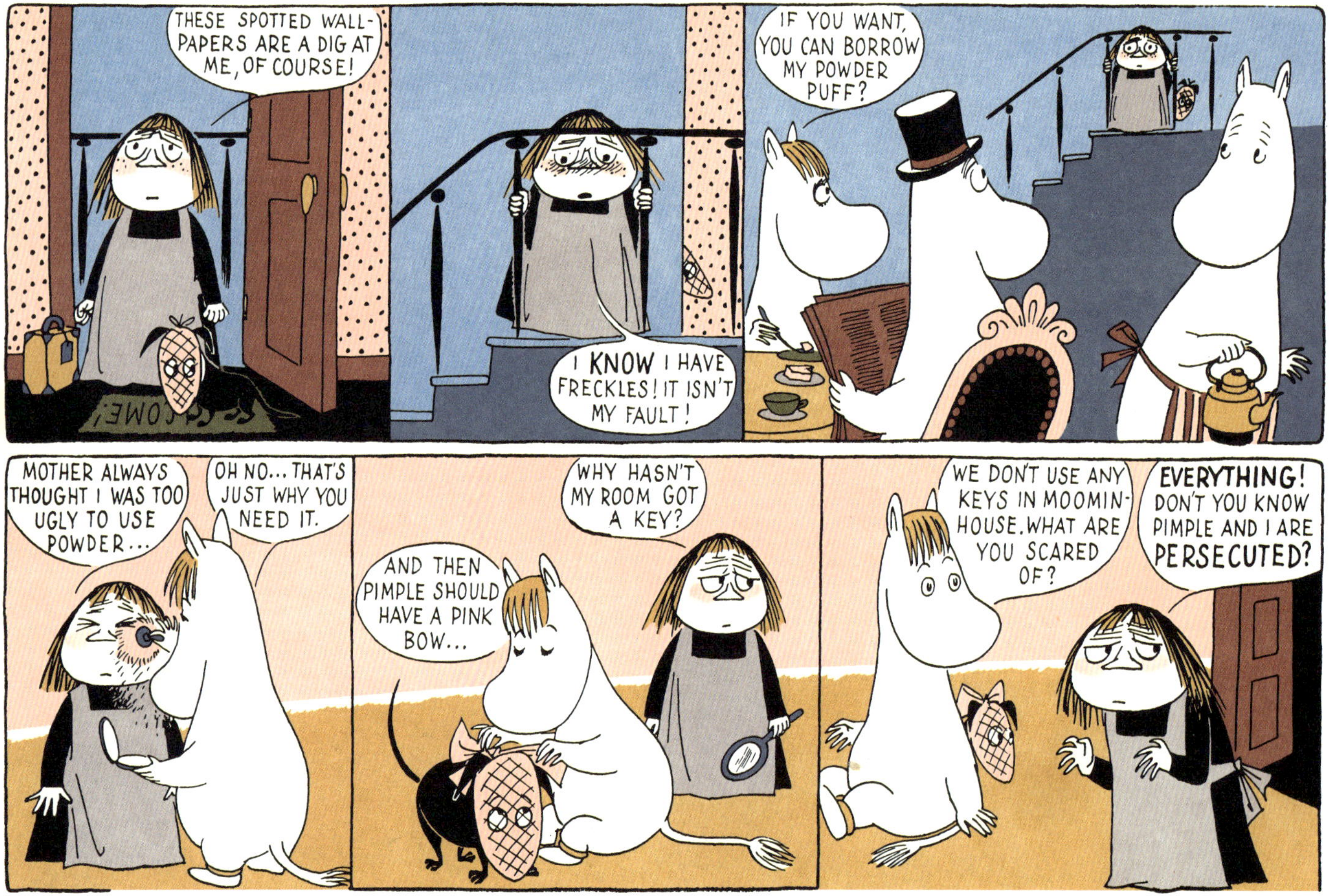
THESE SPOTTED WALL-PAPERS ARE A DIG AT ME, OF COURSE!
I KNOW I HAVE FRECKLES! IT ISN'T MY FAULT!
IF YOU WANT, YOU CAN BORROW MY POWDER PUFF?
MOTHER ALWAYS THOUGHT I WAS TOO UGLY TO USE POWDER...
OH NO... THAT'S JUST WHY YOU NEED IT.
AND THEN PIMPLE SHOULD HAVE A PINK BOW...
WHY HASN'T MY ROOM GOT A KEY?
WE DON'T USE ANY KEYS IN MOOMIN-HOUSE. WHAT ARE YOU SCARED OF?
EVERYTHING! DON'T YOU KNOW PIMPLE AND I ARE PERSECUTED?

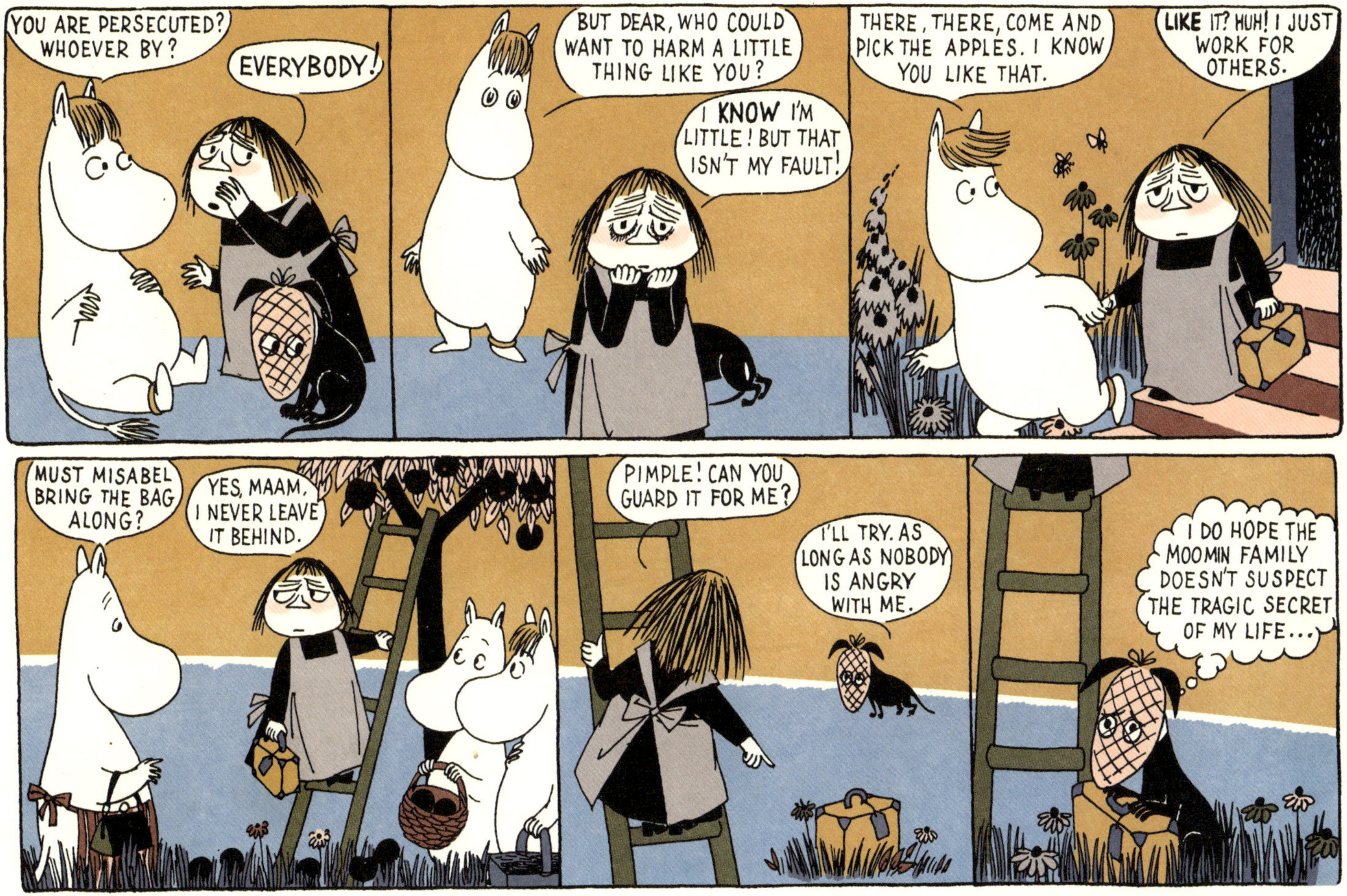
YOU ARE PERSECUTED? WHOEVER BY?
EVERYBODY!
BUT DEAR, WHO COULD WANT TO HARM A LITTLE THING LIKE YOU?
I KNOW I'M LITTLE! BUT THAT ISN'T MY FAULT!
THERE, THERE, COME AND PICK THE APPLES. I KNOW YOU LIKE THAT.
LIKE IT? HUH! I JUST WORK FOR OTHERS.
MUST MISABEL BRING THE BAG ALONG?
YES, MAAM, I NEVER LEAVE IT BEHIND.
PIMPLE! CAN YOU GUARD IT FOR ME?
I'LL TRY. AS LONG AS NOBODY IS ANGRY WITH ME.
I DO HOPE THE MOOMIN FAMILY DOESN'T SUSPECT THE TRAGIC SECRET OF MY LIFE...

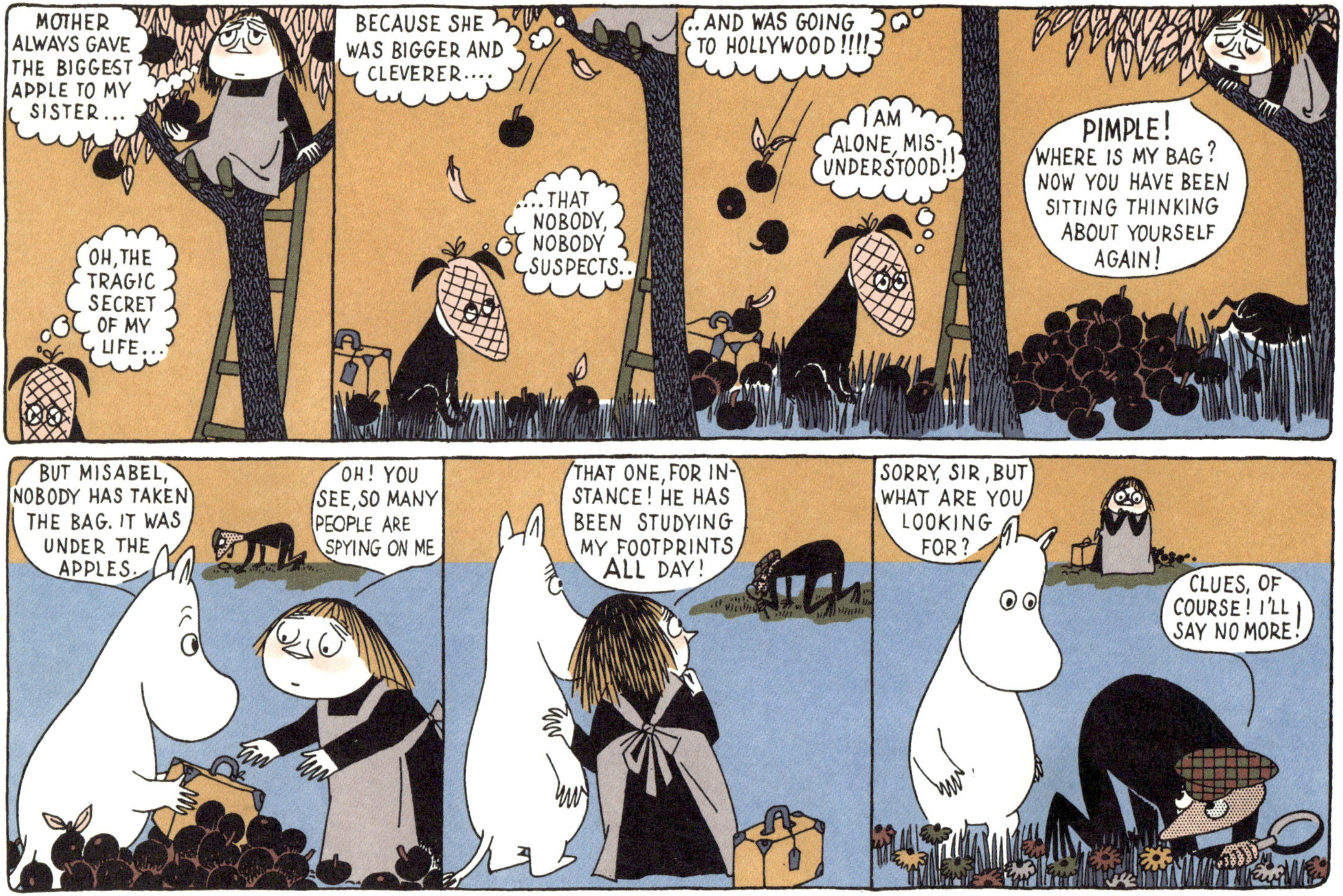
MOTHER ALWAYS GAVE THE BIGGEST APPLE TO MY SISTER...
OH, THE TRAGIC SECRET OF MY LIFE...
BECAUSE SHE WAS BIGGER AND CLEVERER....
...THAT NOBODY, NOBODY SUSPECTS..
..AND WAS GOING TO HOLLYWOOD!!!!
I AM ALONE, MIS-UNDERSTOOD!!
PIMPLE! WHERE IS MY BAG? NOW YOU HAVE BEEN SITTING THINKING ABOUT YOURSELF AGAIN!
BUT MISABEL, NOBODY HAS TAKEN THE BAG. IT WAS UNDER THE APPLES.
OH! YOU SEE, SO MANY PEOPLE ARE SPYING ON ME
THAT ONE, FOR INSTANCE! HE HAS BEEN STUDYING MY FOOTPRINTS ALL DAY!
SORRY, SIR, BUT WHAT ARE YOU LOOKING FOR?
CLUES, OF COURSE! I'LL SAY NO MORE!

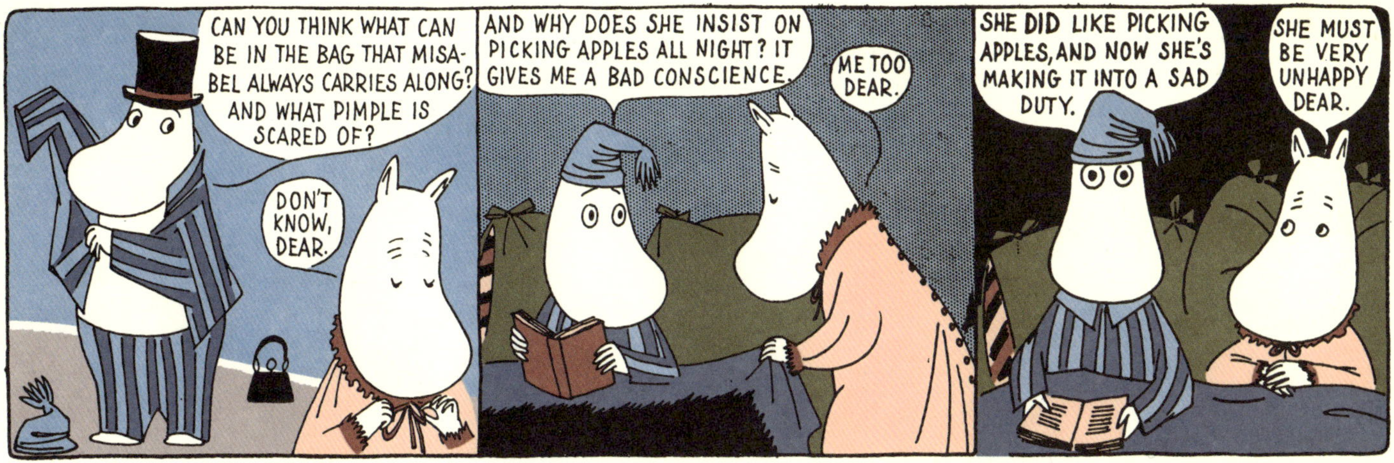
CAN YOU THINK WHAT CAN BE IN THE BAG THAT MISA-BEL ALWAYS CARRIES ALONG? AND WHAT PIMPLE IS SCARED OF?
DON'T KNOW, DEAR.
AND WHY DOES SHE INSIST ON PICKING APPLES ALL NIGHT? IT GIVES ME A BAD CONSCIENCE.
ME TOO DEAR.
SHE DID LIKE PICKING APPLES, AND NOW SHE'S MAKING IT INTO A SAD DUTY.
SHE MUST BE VERY UNHAPPY DEAR.

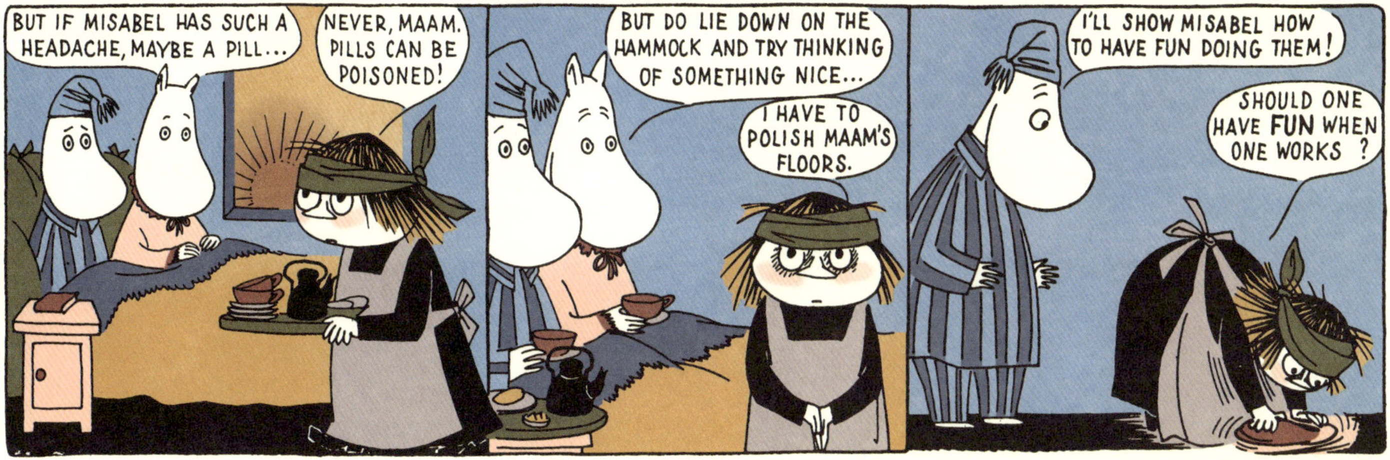
BUT IF MISABEL HAS SUCH A HEADACHE, MAYBE A PILL...
NEVER, MAAM. PILLS CAN BE POISONED!
BUT DO LIE DOWN ON THE HAMMOCK AND TRY THINKING OF SOMETHING NICE...
I HAVE TO POLISH MAAM'S FLOORS.
I'LL SHOW MISABEL HOW TO HAVE FUN DOING THEM!
SHOULD ONE HAVE FUN WHEN ONE WORKS ?

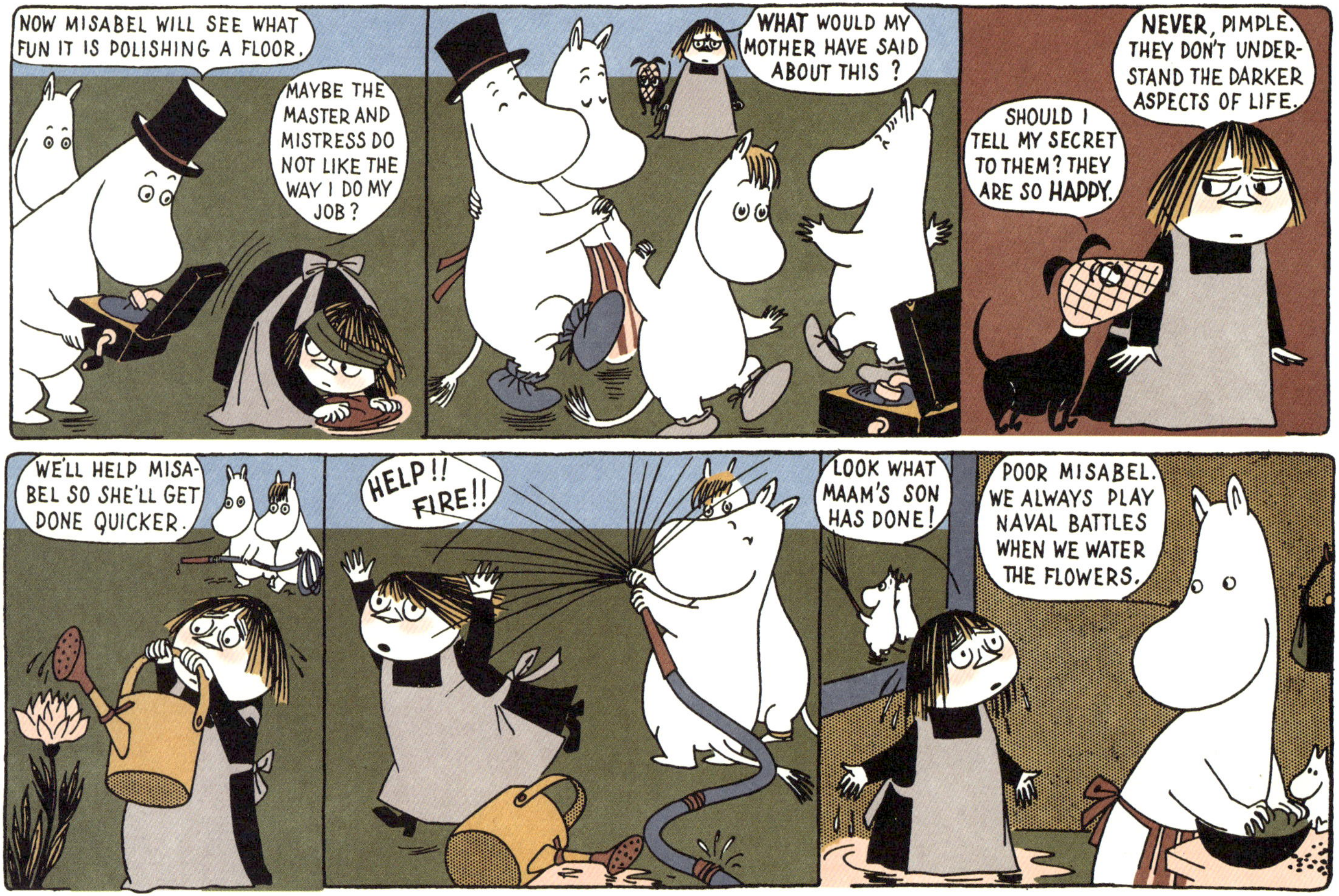
NOW MISABEL WILL SEE WHAT FUN IT IS POLISHING A FLOOR.
MAYBE THE MASTER AND MISTRESS DO NOT LIKE THE WAY I DO MY JOB?
WHAT WOULD MY MOTHER HAVE SAID ABOUT THIS ?
SHOULD I TELL MY SECRET TO THEM? THEY ARE SO HAPPY.
NEVER, PIMPLE. THEY DON'T UNDERSTAND THE DARKER ASPECTS OF LIFE.
WE'LL HELP MISABEL SO SHE'LL GET DONE QUICKER.
HELP!! FIRE!!
LOOK WHAT MAAM'S SON HAS DONE!
POOR MISABEL. WE ALWAYS PLAY NAVAL BATTLES WHEN WE WATER THE FLOWERS.

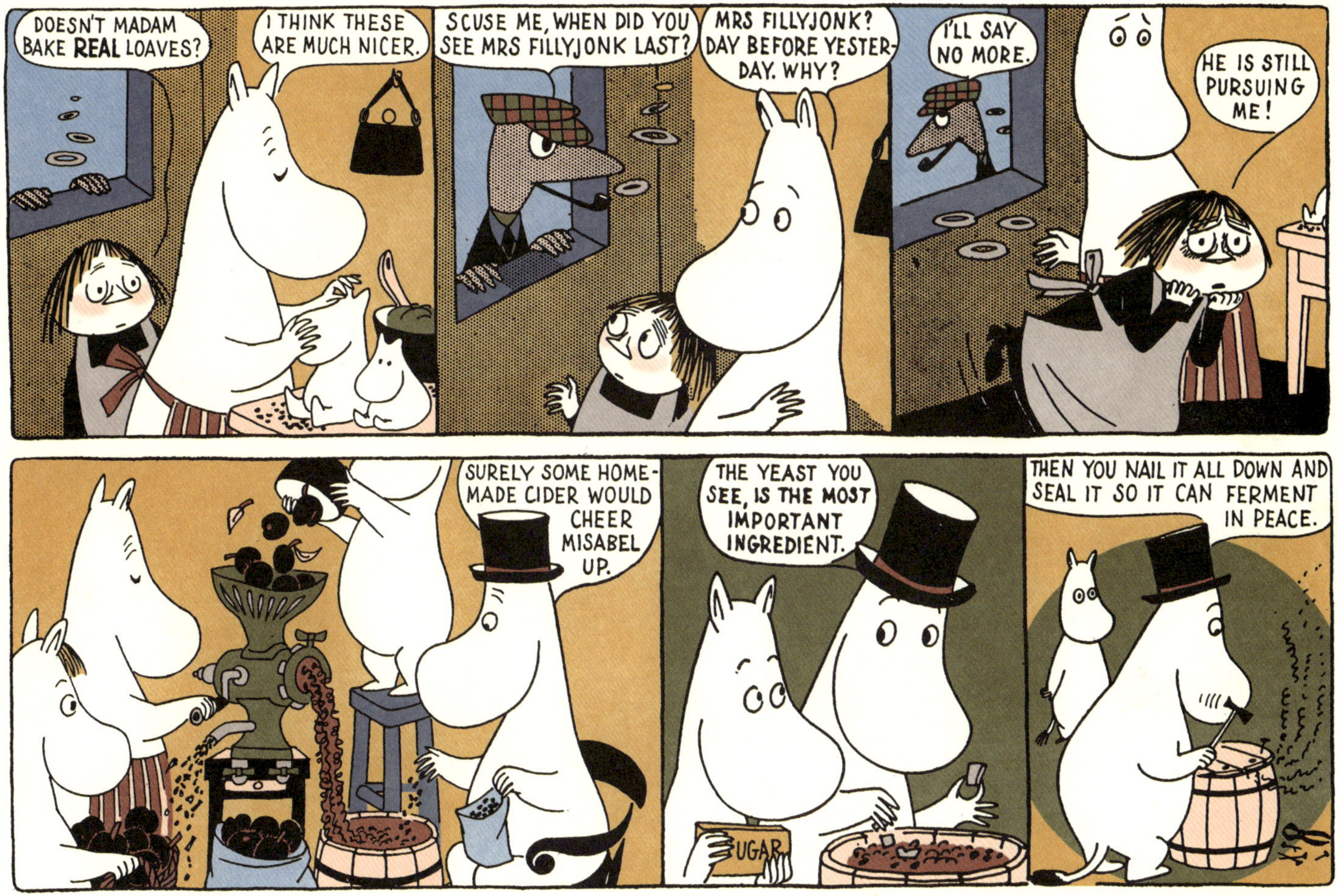
DOESN'T MADAM BAKE **REAL** LOAVES?
I THINK THESE ARE MUCH NICER.
SCUSE ME, WHEN DID YOU SEE MRS FILLYJONK LAST?
MRS FILLYJONK? DAY BEFORE YESTERDAY. WHY?
I'LL SAY NO MORE.
HE IS STILL PURSUING ME!
SURELY SOME HOME-MADE CIDER WOULD CHEER MISABEL UP.
THE YEAST YOU SEE, IS THE MOST IMPORTANT INGREDIENT.
SUGAR
THEN YOU NAIL IT ALL DOWN AND SEAL IT SO IT CAN FERMENT IN PEACE.

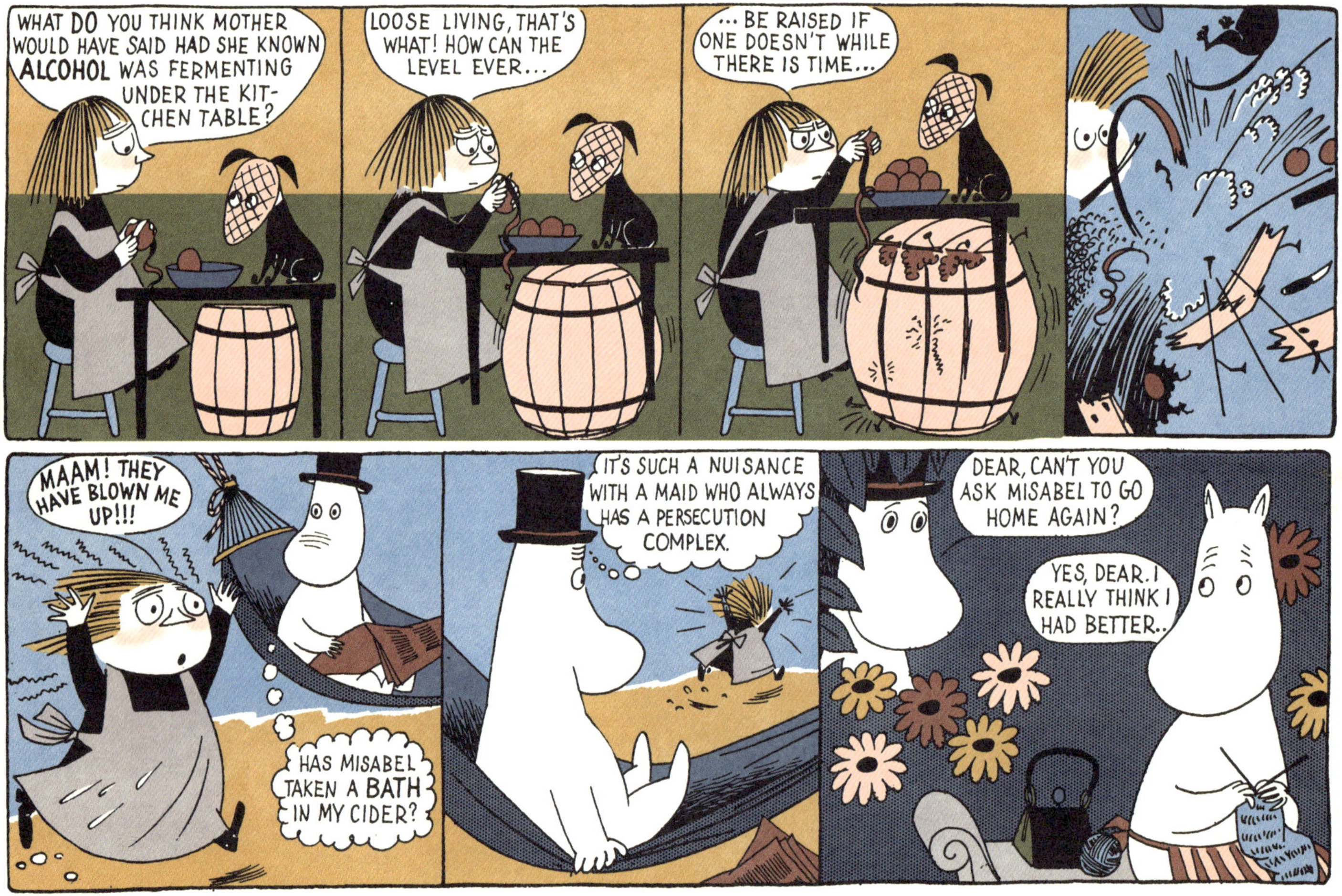
WHAT DO YOU THINK MOTHER WOULD HAVE SAID HAD SHE KNOWN ALCOHOL WAS FERMENTING UNDER THE KIT-CHEN TABLE?
LOOSE LIVING, THAT'S WHAT! HOW CAN THE LEVEL EVER...
... BE RAISED IF ONE DOESN'T WHILE THERE IS TIME...
MAAM! THEY HAVE BLOWN ME UP!!!
HAS MISABEL TAKEN A BATH IN MY CIDER?
IT'S SUCH A NUISANCE WITH A MAID WHO ALWAYS HAS A PERSECUTION COMPLEX.
DEAR, CAN'T YOU ASK MISABEL TO GO HOME AGAIN?
YES, DEAR. I REALLY THINK I HAD BETTER..

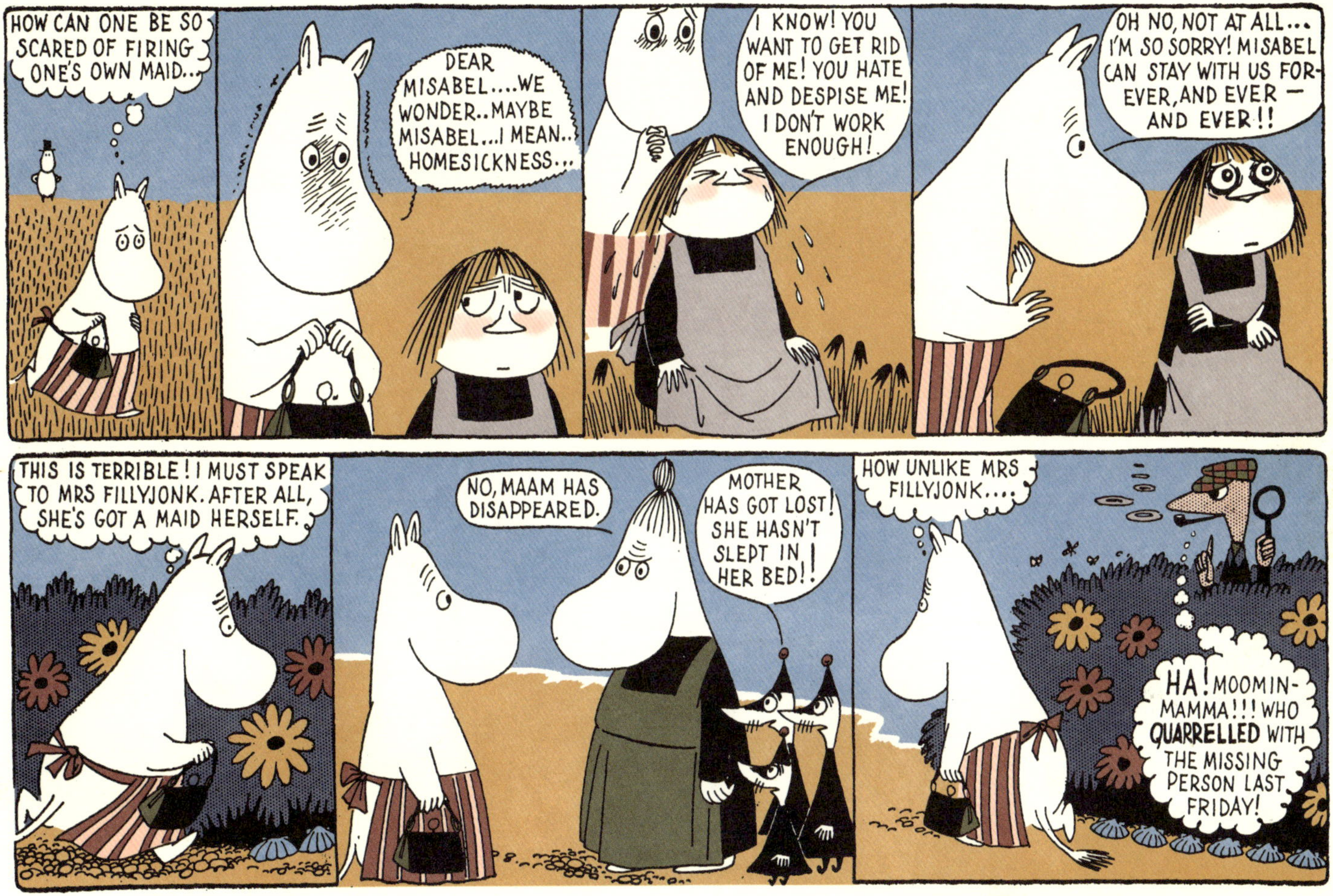
HOW CAN ONE BE SO SCARED OF FIRING ONE'S OWN MAID...
DEAR MISABEL....WE WONDER..MAYBE MISABEL...I MEAN.. HOMESICKNESS...
I KNOW! YOU WANT TO GET RID OF ME! YOU HATE AND DESPISE ME! I DON'T WORK ENOUGH!
OH NO, NOT AT ALL... I'M SO SORRY! MISABEL CAN STAY WITH US FOR-EVER, AND EVER — AND EVER!!
THIS IS TERRIBLE! I MUST SPEAK TO MRS FILLYJONK. AFTER ALL, SHE'S GOT A MAID HERSELF.
NO, MAAM HAS DISAPPEARED.
MOTHER HAS GOT LOST! SHE HASN'T SLEPT IN HER BED!!
HOW UNLIKE MRS FILLYJONK....
HA! MOOMIN-MAMMA!!! WHO QUARRELLED WITH THE MISSING PERSON LAST FRIDAY!

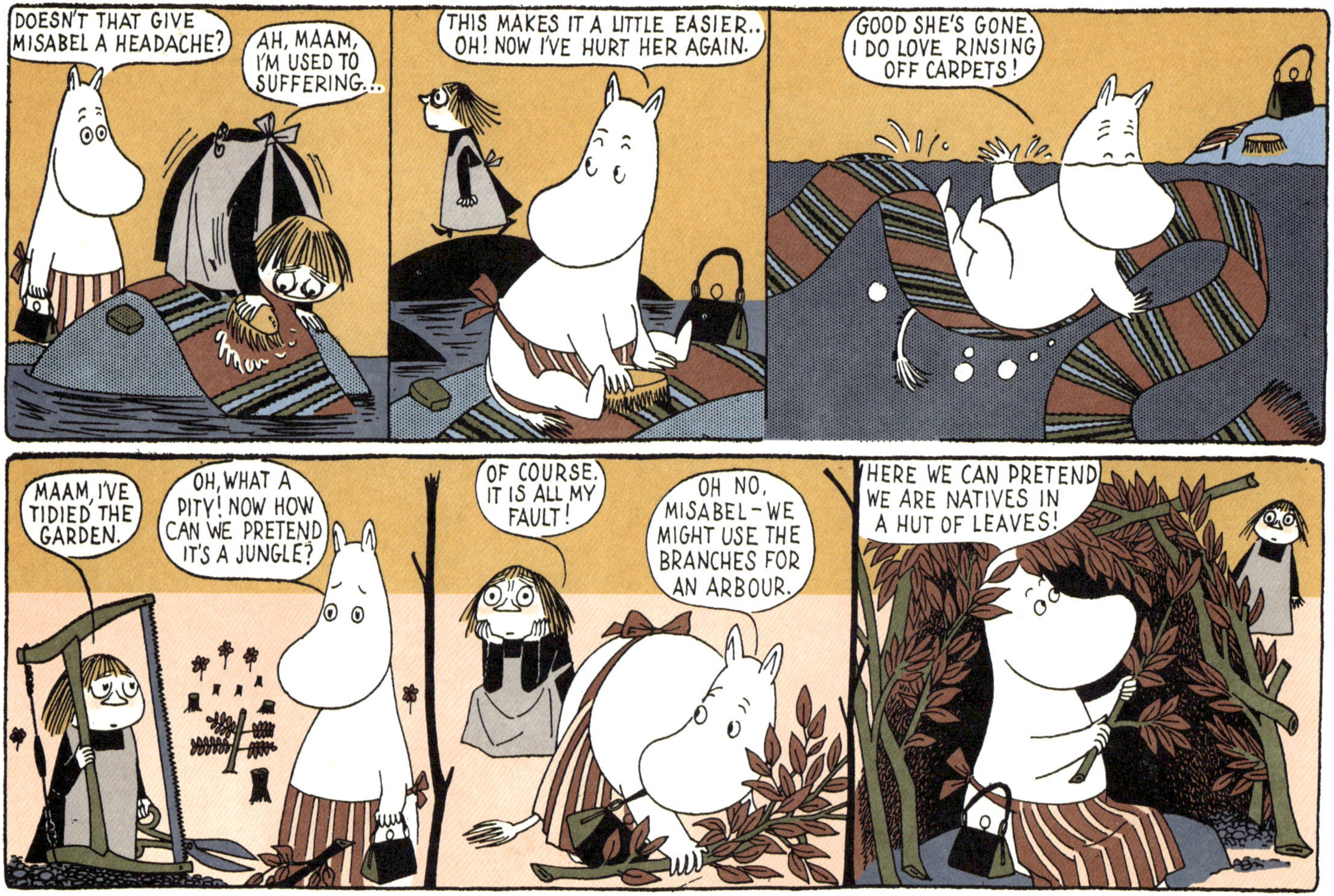
DOESN'T THAT GIVE MISABEL A HEADACHE?
AH, MAAM, I'M USED TO SUFFERING...
THIS MAKES IT A LITTLE EASIER.. OH! NOW I'VE HURT HER AGAIN.
GOOD SHE'S GONE. I DO LOVE RINSING OFF CARPETS!
MAAM, I'VE TIDIED THE GARDEN.
OH, WHAT A PITY! NOW HOW CAN WE PRETEND IT'S A JUNGLE?
OF COURSE. IT IS ALL MY FAULT!
OH NO, MISABEL - WE MIGHT USE THE BRANCHES FOR AN ARBOUR.
HERE WE CAN PRETEND WE ARE NATIVES IN A HUT OF LEAVES!

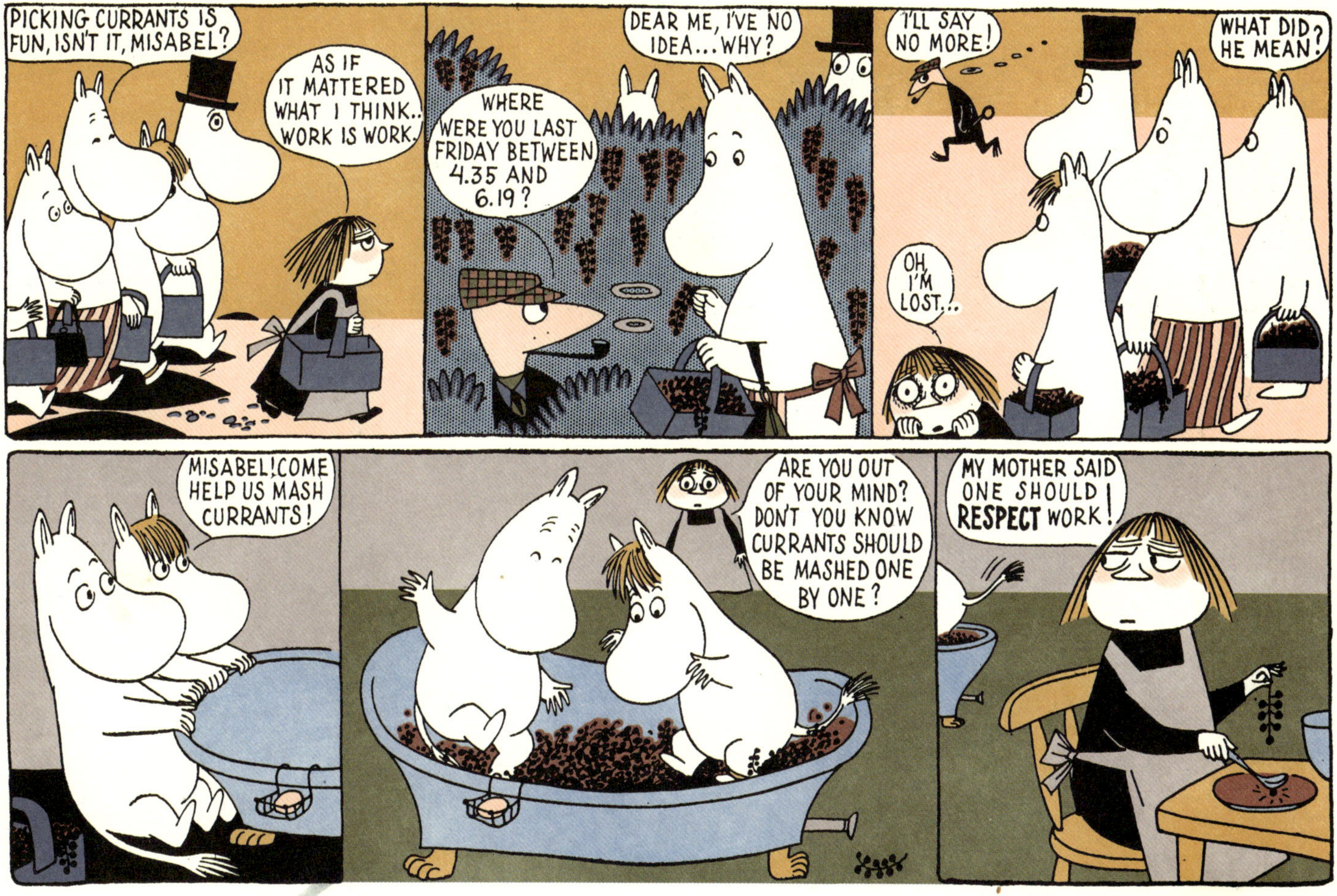

PICKING CURRANTS IS FUN, ISN'T IT, MISABEL?
AS IF IT MATTERED WHAT I THINK.. WORK IS WORK.
WHERE WERE YOU LAST FRIDAY BETWEEN 4.35 AND 6.19?
DEAR ME, I'VE NO IDEA... WHY?
I'LL SAY NO MORE!
WHAT DID HE MEAN?
OH, I'M LOST...
MISABEL! COME HELP US MASH CURRANTS!
ARE YOU OUT OF YOUR MIND? DON'T YOU KNOW CURRANTS SHOULD BE MASHED ONE BY ONE?
MY MOTHER SAID ONE SHOULD RESPECT WORK!

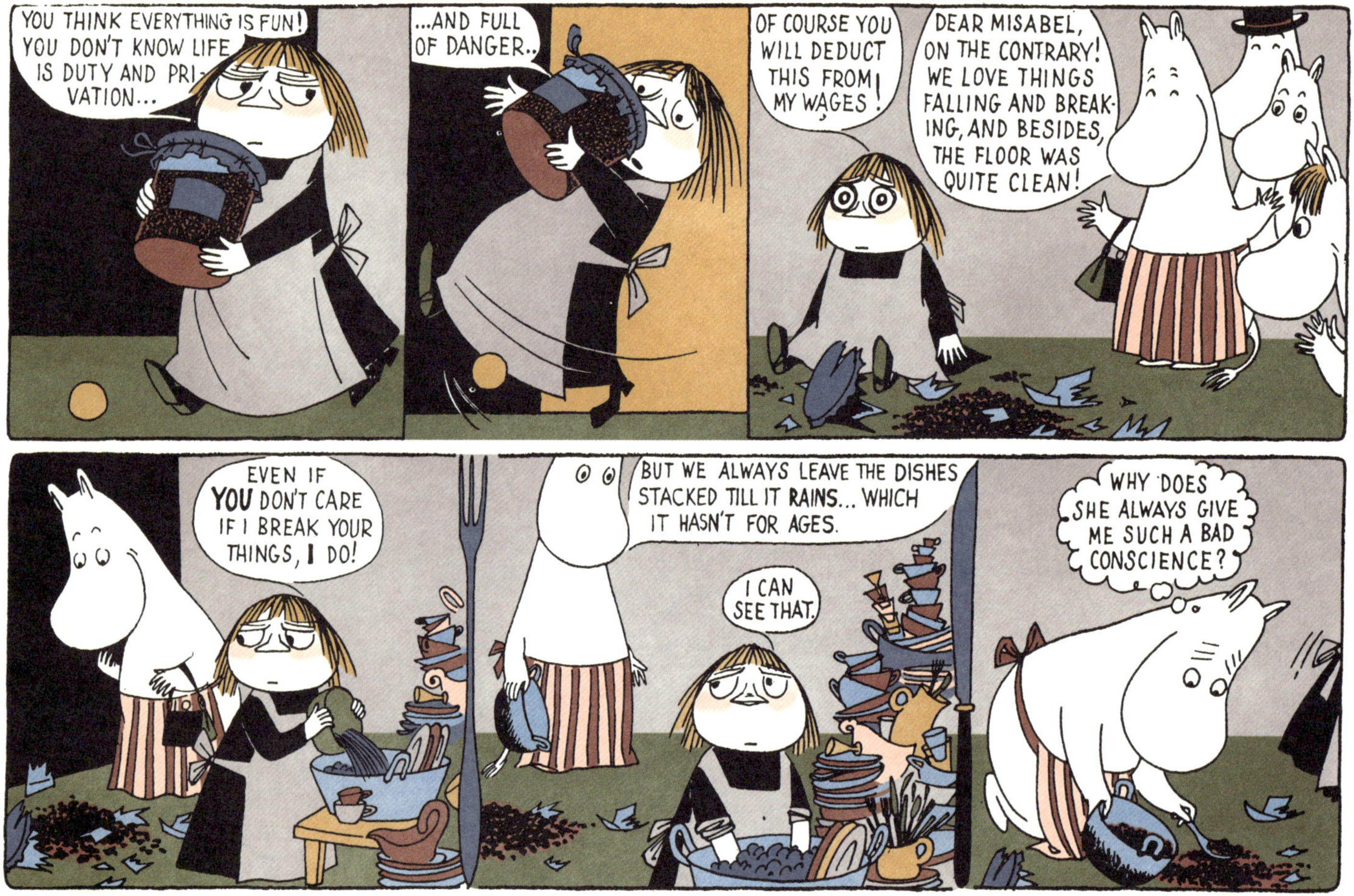
YOU THINK EVERYTHING IS FUN! YOU DON'T KNOW LIFE IS DUTY AND PRI-VATION...
...AND FULL OF DANGER..
OF COURSE YOU WILL DEDUCT THIS FROM MY WAGES!
DEAR MISABEL, ON THE CONTRARY! WE LOVE THINGS FALLING AND BREAK-ING, AND BESIDES, THE FLOOR WAS QUITE CLEAN!
EVEN IF YOU DON'T CARE IF I BREAK YOUR THINGS, I DO!
BUT WE ALWAYS LEAVE THE DISHES STACKED TILL IT RAINS... WHICH IT HASN'T FOR AGES.
I CAN SEE THAT.
WHY DOES SHE ALWAYS GIVE ME SUCH A BAD CONSCIENCE?

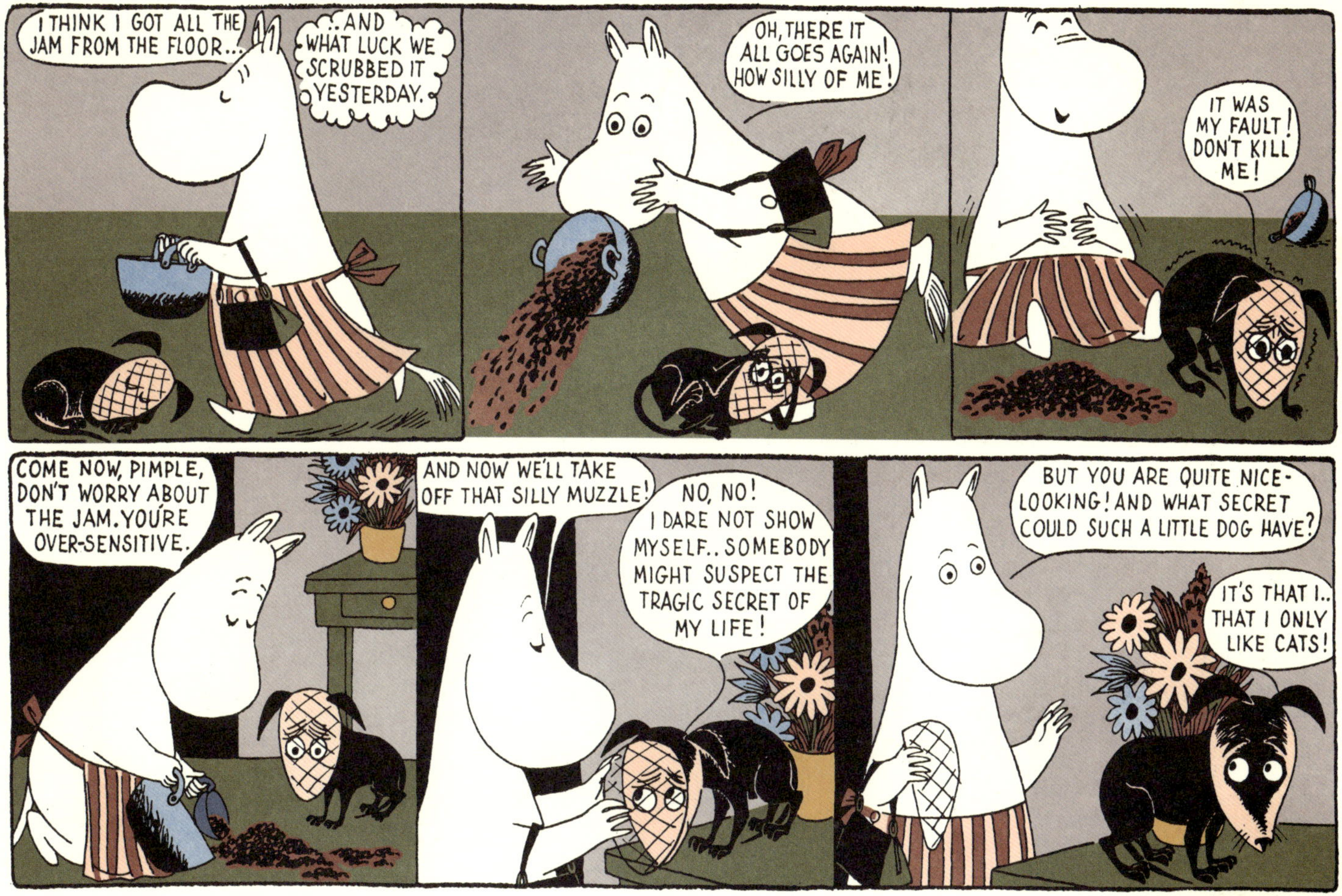
I THINK I GOT ALL THE JAM FROM THE FLOOR...
..AND WHAT LUCK WE SCRUBBED IT YESTERDAY.
OH, THERE IT ALL GOES AGAIN! HOW SILLY OF ME!
IT WAS MY FAULT! DON'T KILL ME!
COME NOW, PIMPLE, DON'T WORRY ABOUT THE JAM. YOU'RE OVER-SENSITIVE.
AND NOW WE'LL TAKE OFF THAT SILLY MUZZLE!
NO, NO! I DARE NOT SHOW MYSELF.. SOMEBODY MIGHT SUSPECT THE TRAGIC SECRET OF MY LIFE!
BUT YOU ARE QUITE NICE-LOOKING! AND WHAT SECRET COULD SUCH A LITTLE DOG HAVE?
IT'S THAT I.. THAT I ONLY LIKE CATS!

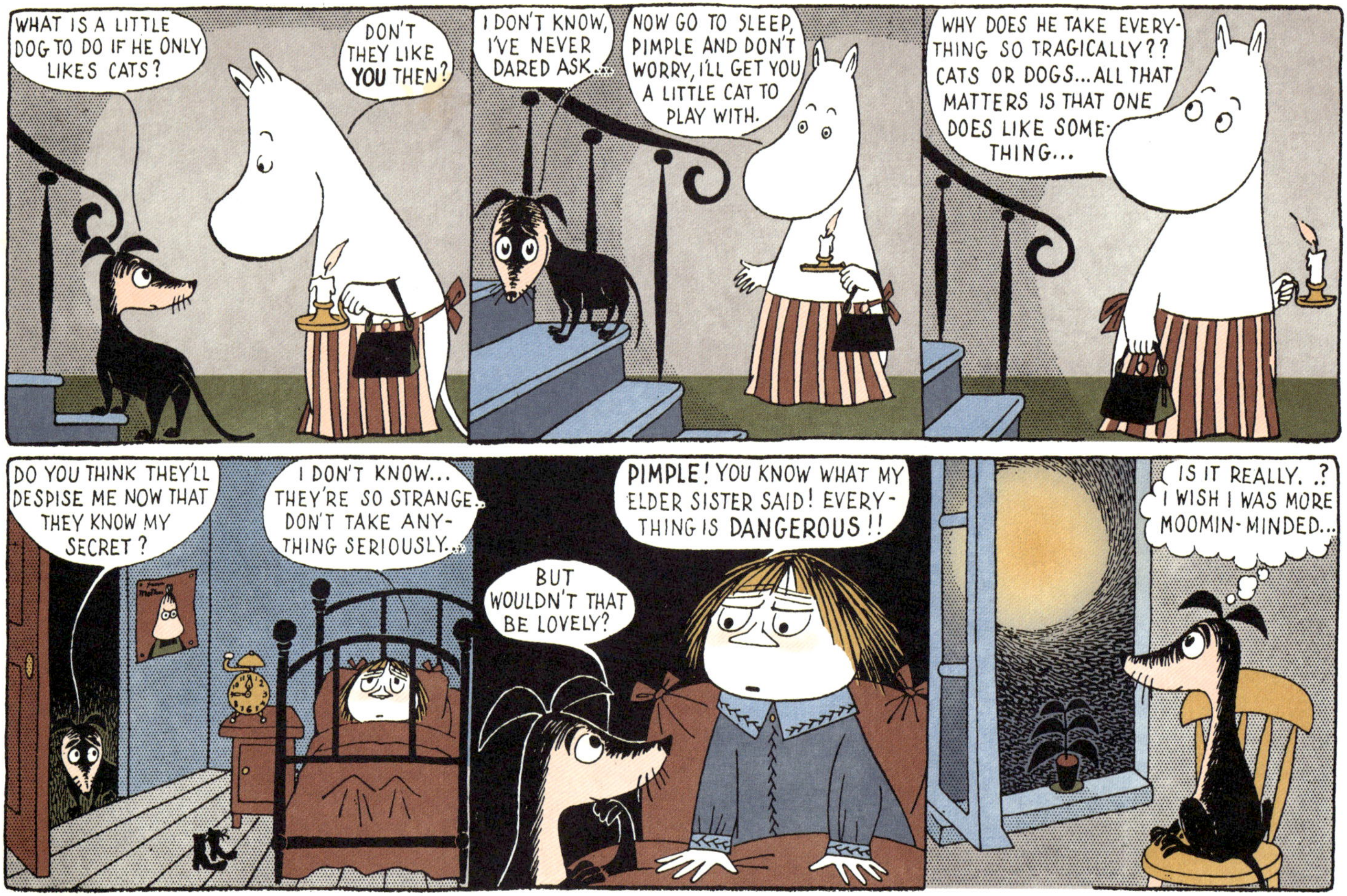
WHAT IS A LITTLE DOG TO DO IF HE ONLY LIKES CATS?
DON'T THEY LIKE YOU THEN?
I DON'T KNOW, I'VE NEVER DARED ASK...
NOW GO TO SLEEP, PIMPLE AND DON'T WORRY, I'LL GET YOU A LITTLE CAT TO PLAY WITH.
WHY DOES HE TAKE EVERYTHING SO TRAGICALLY?? CATS OR DOGS... ALL THAT MATTERS IS THAT ONE DOES LIKE SOMETHING...
DO YOU THINK THEY'LL DESPISE ME NOW THAT THEY KNOW MY SECRET?
I DON'T KNOW... THEY'RE SO STRANGE.. DON'T TAKE ANYTHING SERIOUSLY...
PIMPLE! YOU KNOW WHAT MY ELDER SISTER SAID! EVERYTHING IS DANGEROUS!!
BUT WOULDN'T THAT BE LOVELY?
IS IT REALLY. .? I WISH I WAS MORE MOOMIN-MINDED...

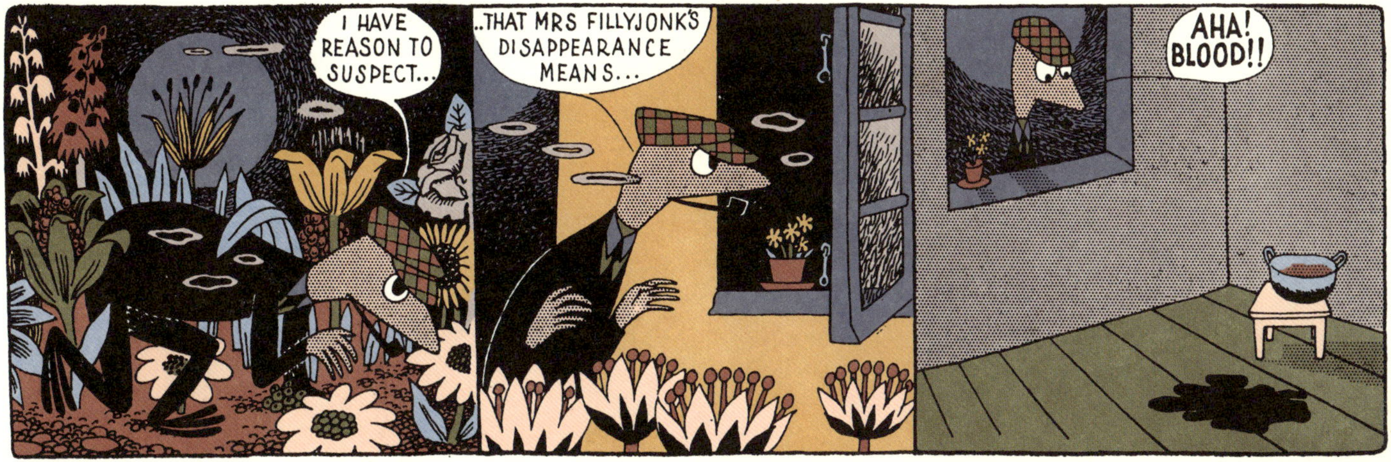
I HAVE REASON TO SUSPECT...
..THAT MRS FILLYJONK'S DISAPPEARANCE MEANS...
AHA! BLOOD!!

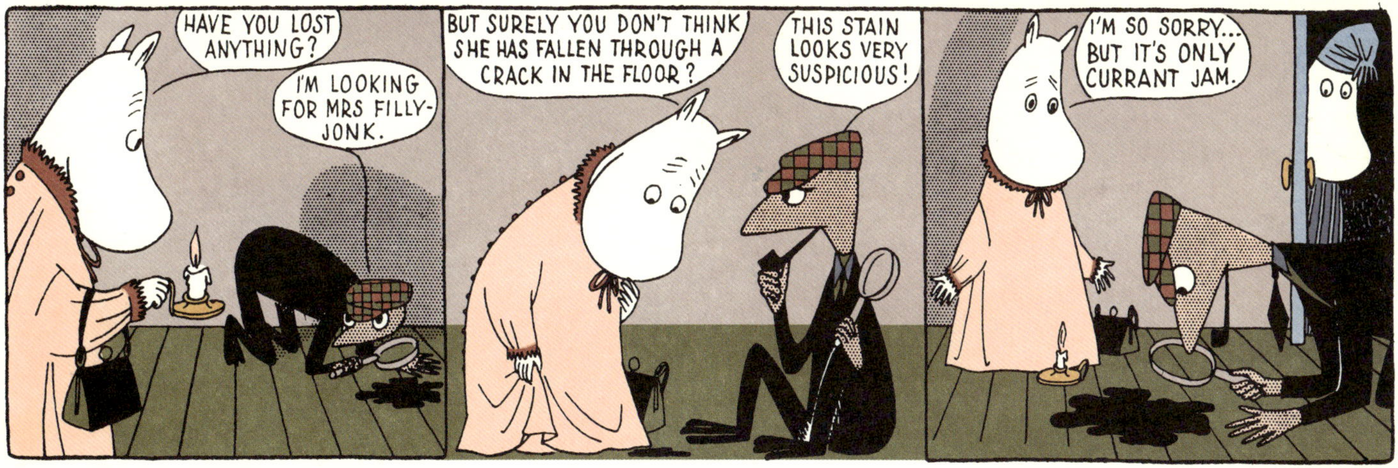
HAVE YOU LOST ANYTHING?
I'M LOOKING FOR MRS FILLY-JONK.
BUT SURELY YOU DON'T THINK SHE HAS FALLEN THROUGH A CRACK IN THE FLOOR?
THIS STAIN LOOKS VERY SUSPICIOUS!
I'M SO SORRY... BUT IT'S ONLY CURRANT JAM.

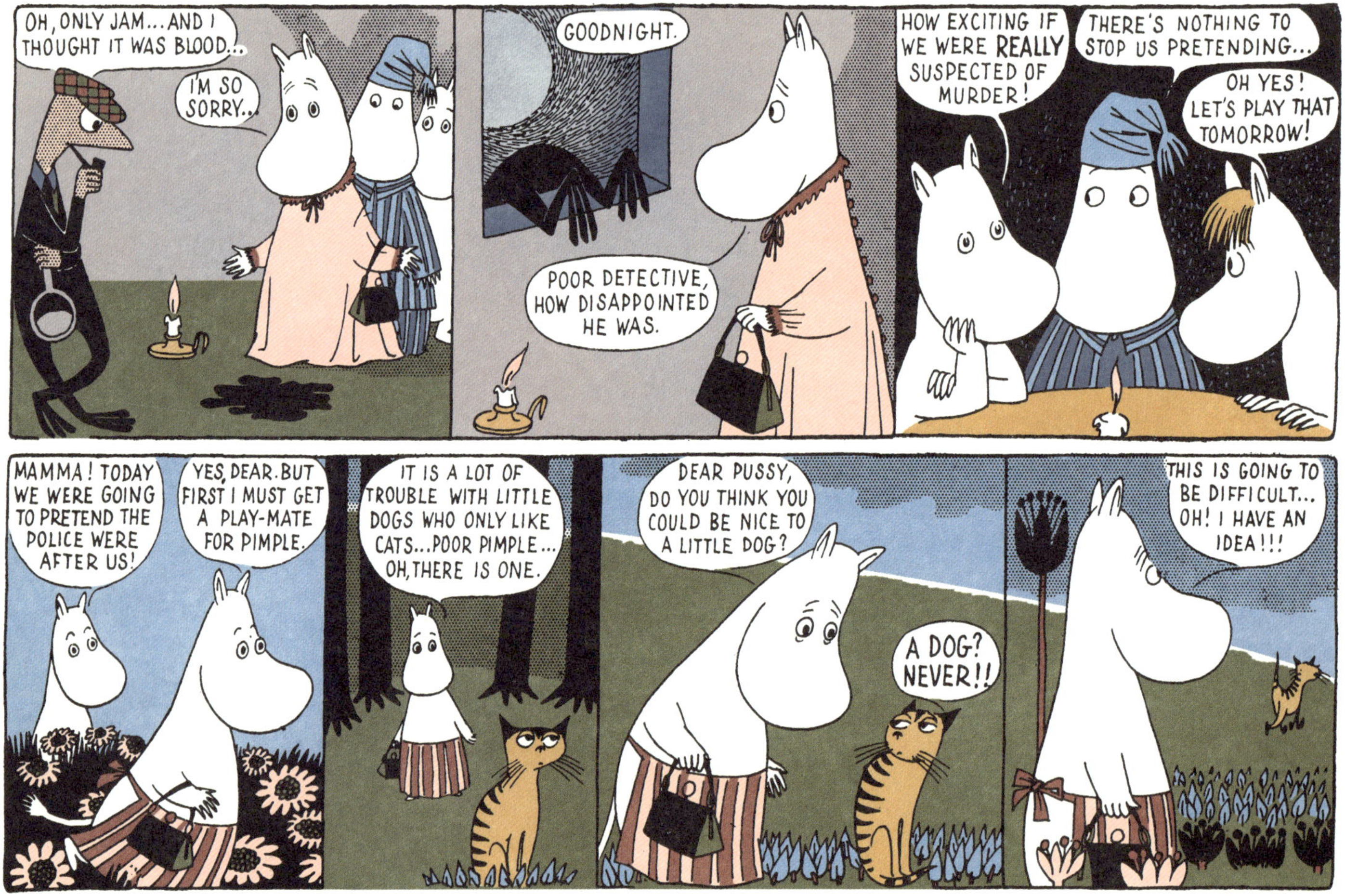
OH, ONLY JAM...AND I THOUGHT IT WAS BLOOD...
I'M SO SORRY...
GOODNIGHT.
POOR DETECTIVE, HOW DISAPPOINTED HE WAS.
HOW EXCITING IF WE WERE REALLY SUSPECTED OF MURDER!
THERE'S NOTHING TO STOP US PRETENDING...
OH YES! LET'S PLAY THAT TOMORROW!
MAMMA! TODAY WE WERE GOING TO PRETEND THE POLICE WERE AFTER US!
YES, DEAR. BUT FIRST I MUST GET A PLAY-MATE FOR PIMPLE.
IT IS A LOT OF TROUBLE WITH LITTLE DOGS WHO ONLY LIKE CATS...POOR PIMPLE... OH, THERE IS ONE.
DEAR PUSSY, DO YOU THINK YOU COULD BE NICE TO A LITTLE DOG?
A DOG? NEVER!!
THIS IS GOING TO BE DIFFICULT... OH! I HAVE AN IDEA!!!

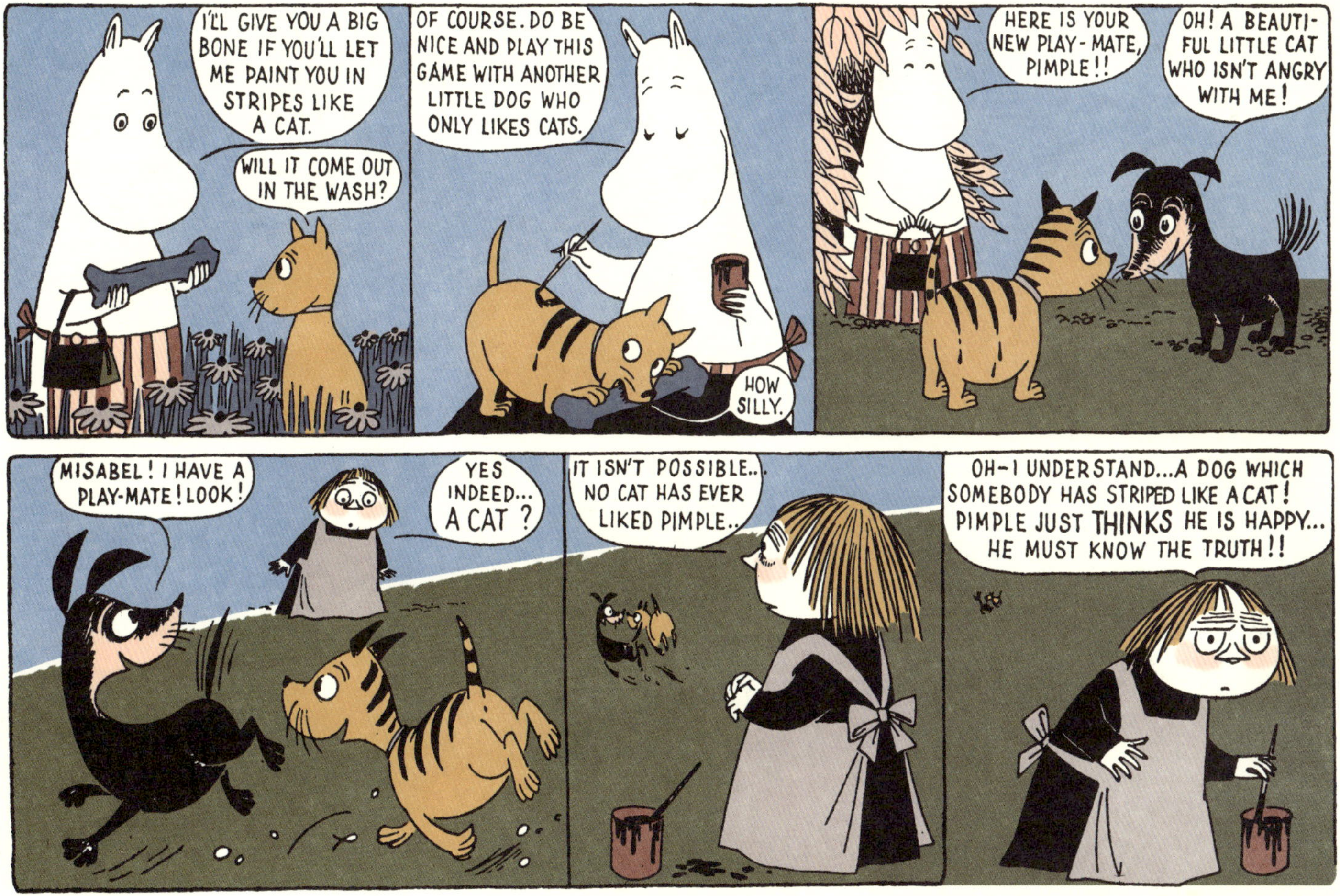
I'LL GIVE YOU A BIG BONE IF YOU'LL LET ME PAINT YOU IN STRIPES LIKE A CAT.
WILL IT COME OUT IN THE WASH?
OF COURSE. DO BE NICE AND PLAY THIS GAME WITH ANOTHER LITTLE DOG WHO ONLY LIKES CATS.
HOW SILLY.
HERE IS YOUR NEW PLAY-MATE, PIMPLE!!
OH! A BEAUTIFUL LITTLE CAT WHO ISN'T ANGRY WITH ME!
MISABEL! I HAVE A PLAY-MATE! LOOK!
YES INDEED... A CAT?
IT ISN'T POSSIBLE... NO CAT HAS EVER LIKED PIMPLE...
OH–I UNDERSTAND...A DOG WHICH SOMEBODY HAS STRIPED LIKE A CAT! PIMPLE JUST THINKS HE IS HAPPY... HE MUST KNOW THE TRUTH!!

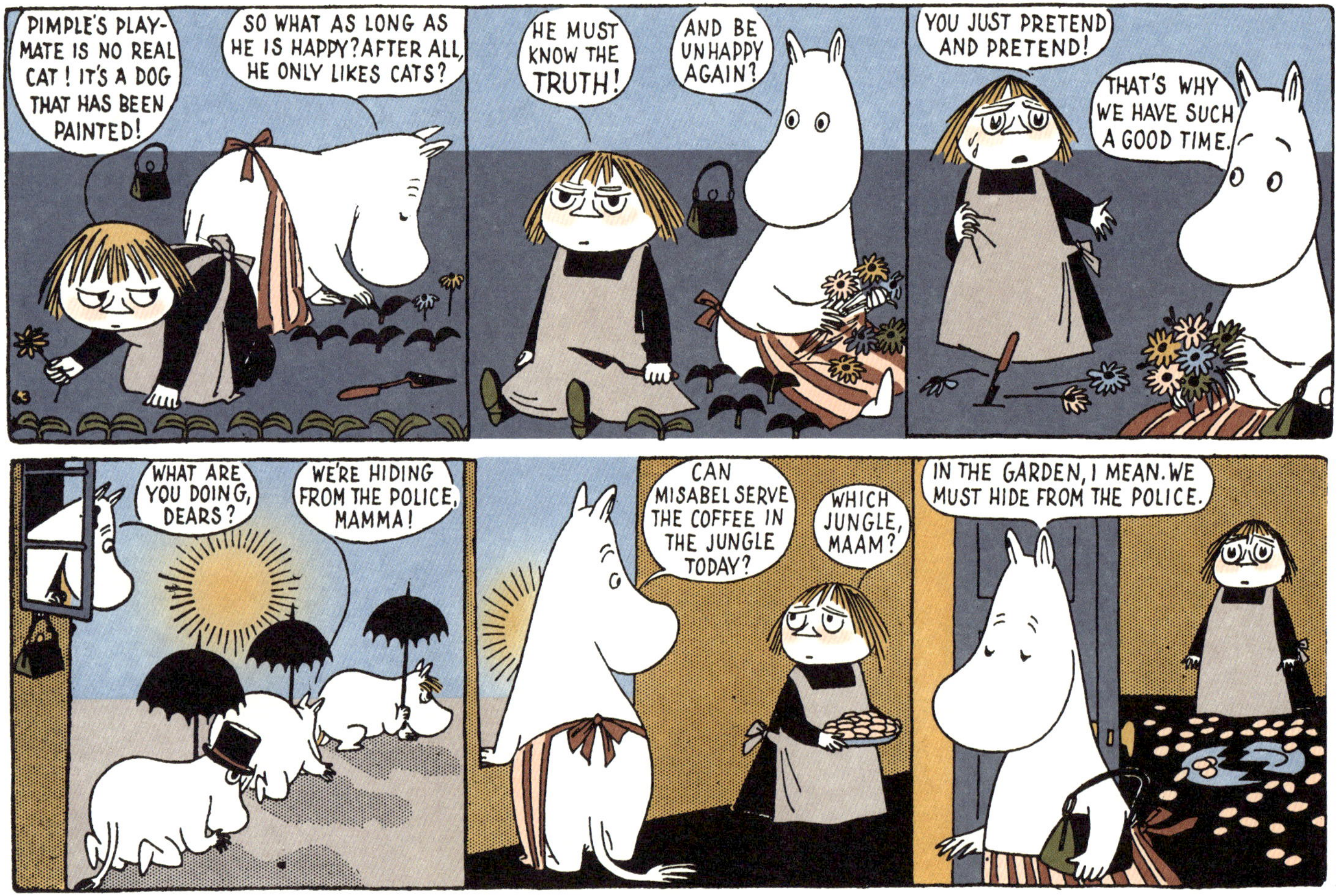
PIMPLE'S PLAYMATE IS NO REAL CAT! IT'S A DOG THAT HAS BEEN PAINTED!
SO WHAT AS LONG AS HE IS HAPPY? AFTER ALL, HE ONLY LIKES CATS?
HE MUST KNOW THE TRUTH!
AND BE UNHAPPY AGAIN?
YOU JUST PRETEND AND PRETEND!
THAT'S WHY WE HAVE SUCH A GOOD TIME.
WHAT ARE YOU DOING, DEARS?
WE'RE HIDING FROM THE POLICE, MAMMA!
CAN MISABEL SERVE THE COFFEE IN THE JUNGLE TODAY?
WHICH JUNGLE, MAAM?
IN THE GARDEN, I MEAN. WE MUST HIDE FROM THE POLICE.

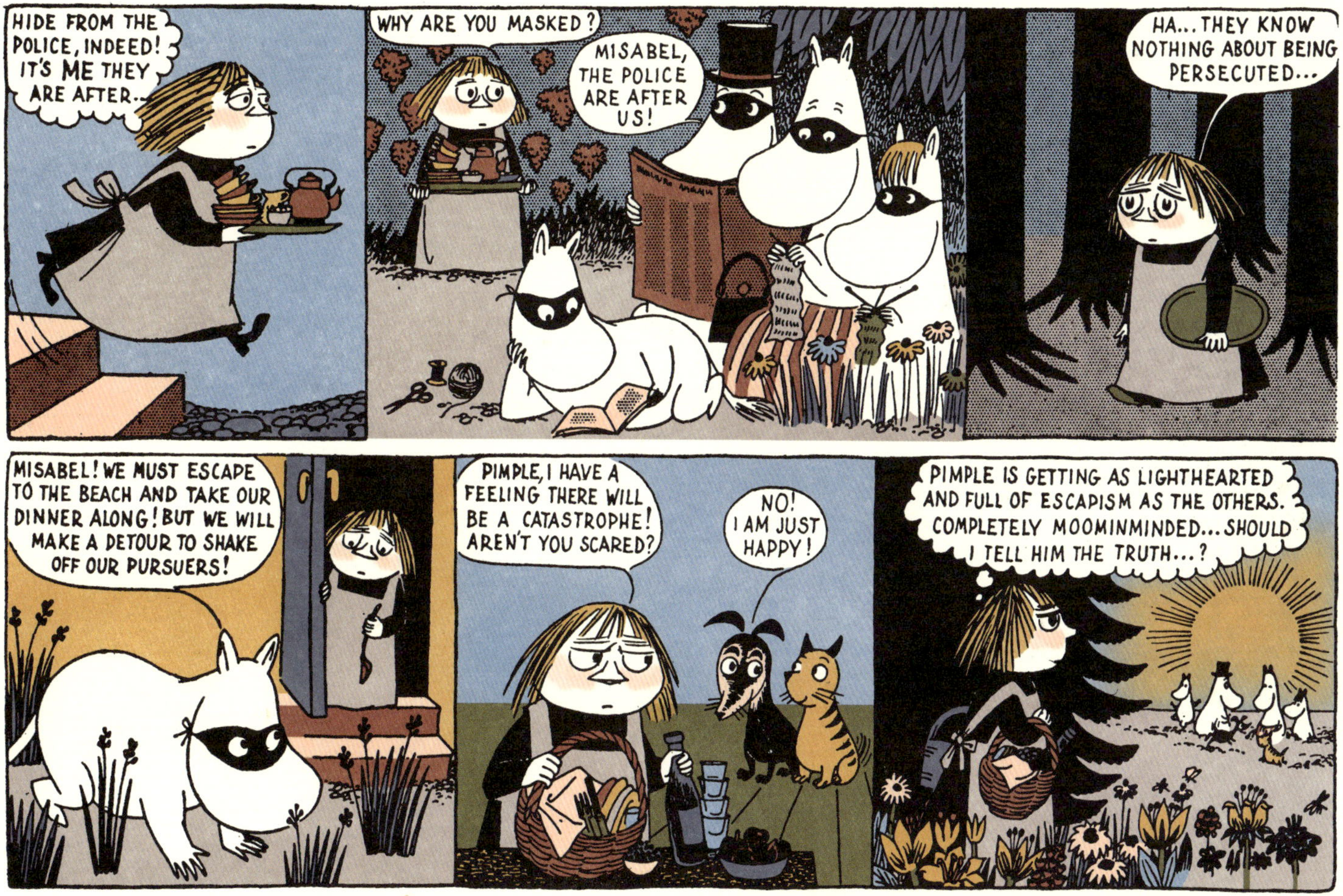
HIDE FROM THE POLICE, INDEED! IT'S ME THEY ARE AFTER...
WHY ARE YOU MASKED?
MISABEL, THE POLICE ARE AFTER US!
HA... THEY KNOW NOTHING ABOUT BEING PERSECUTED...
MISABEL! WE MUST ESCAPE TO THE BEACH AND TAKE OUR DINNER ALONG! BUT WE WILL MAKE A DETOUR TO SHAKE OFF OUR PURSUERS!
PIMPLE, I HAVE A FEELING THERE WILL BE A CATASTROPHE! AREN'T YOU SCARED?
NO! I AM JUST HAPPY!
PIMPLE IS GETTING AS LIGHTHEARTED AND FULL OF ESCAPISM AS THE OTHERS. COMPLETELY MOOMINMINDED... SHOULD I TELL HIM THE TRUTH...?

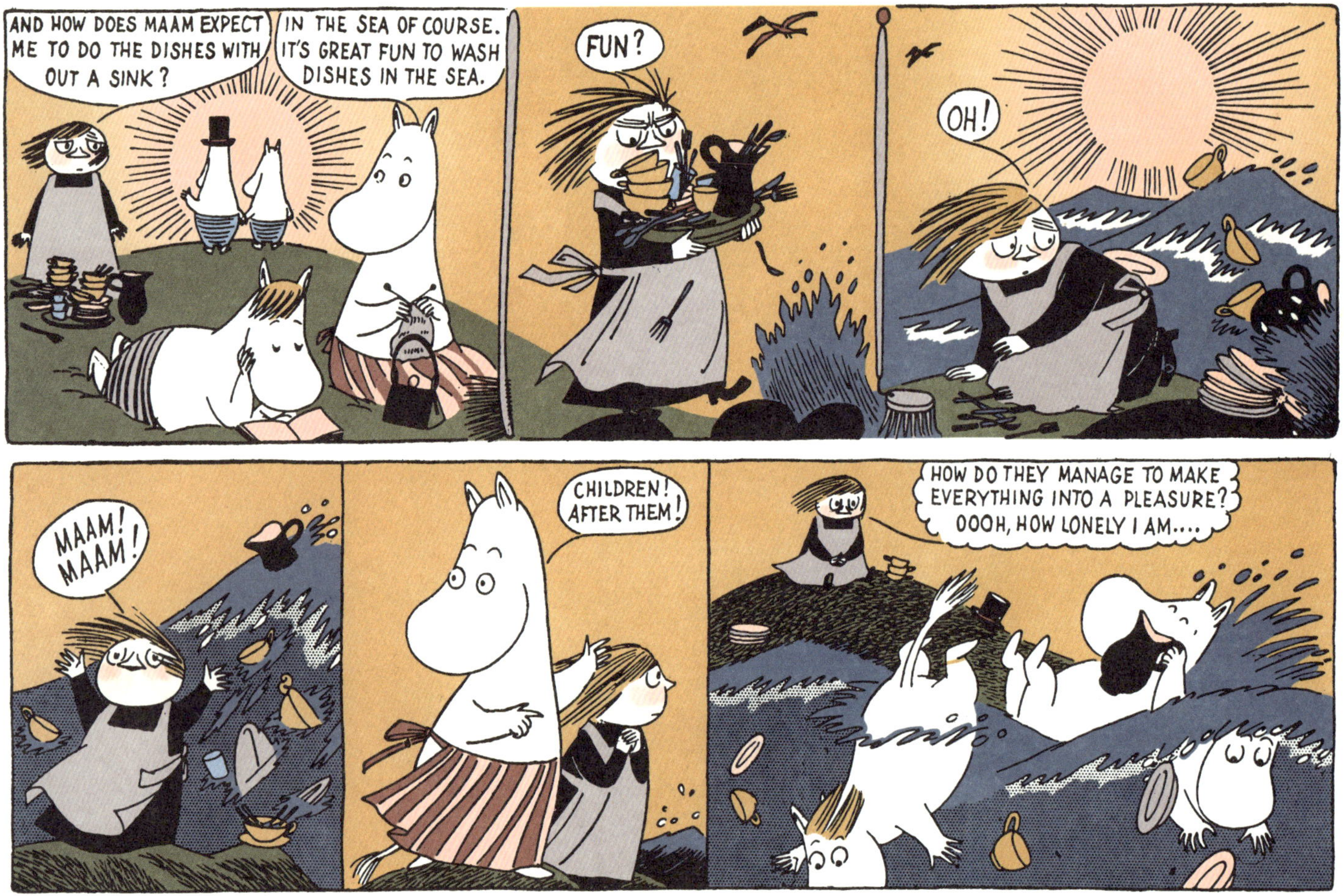
AND HOW DOES MAAM EXPECT ME TO DO THE DISHES WITH OUT A SINK?
IN THE SEA OF COURSE. IT'S GREAT FUN TO WASH DISHES IN THE SEA.
FUN?
OH!
MAAM! MAAM!
CHILDREN! AFTER THEM!
HOW DO THEY MANAGE TO MAKE EVERYTHING INTO A PLEASURE? OOOH, HOW LONELY I AM....

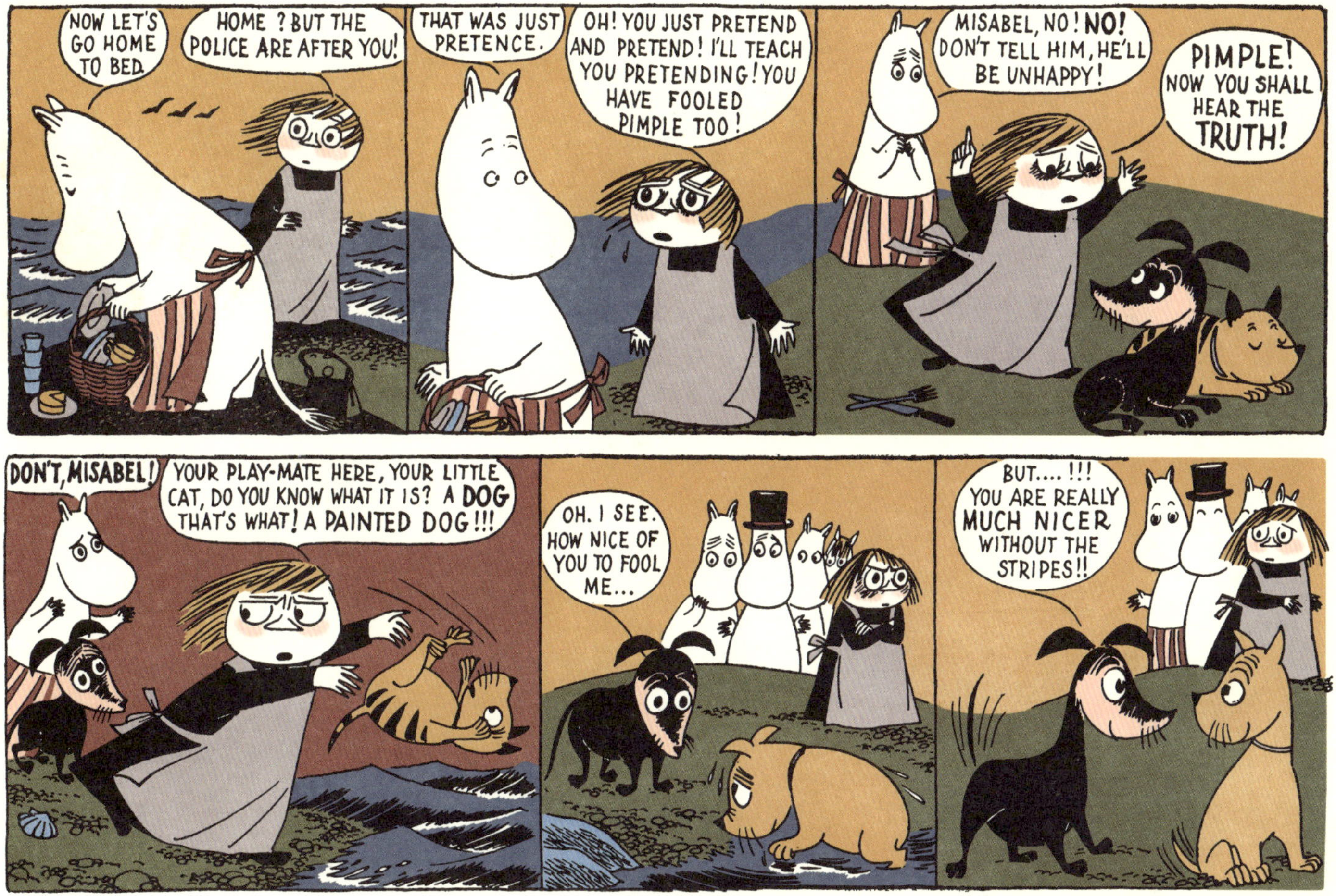
NOW LET'S GO HOME TO BED.
HOME ? BUT THE POLICE ARE AFTER YOU!
THAT WAS JUST PRETENCE.
OH! YOU JUST PRETEND AND PRETEND! I'LL TEACH YOU PRETENDING! YOU HAVE FOOLED PIMPLE TOO!
MISABEL, NO! NO! DON'T TELL HIM, HE'LL BE UNHAPPY!
PIMPLE! NOW YOU SHALL HEAR THE TRUTH!
DON'T, MISABEL!
YOUR PLAY-MATE HERE, YOUR LITTLE CAT, DO YOU KNOW WHAT IT IS? A DOG THAT'S WHAT! A PAINTED DOG!!!
OH. I SEE. HOW NICE OF YOU TO FOOL ME...
BUT.... !!! YOU ARE REALLY MUCH NICER WITHOUT THE STRIPES!!

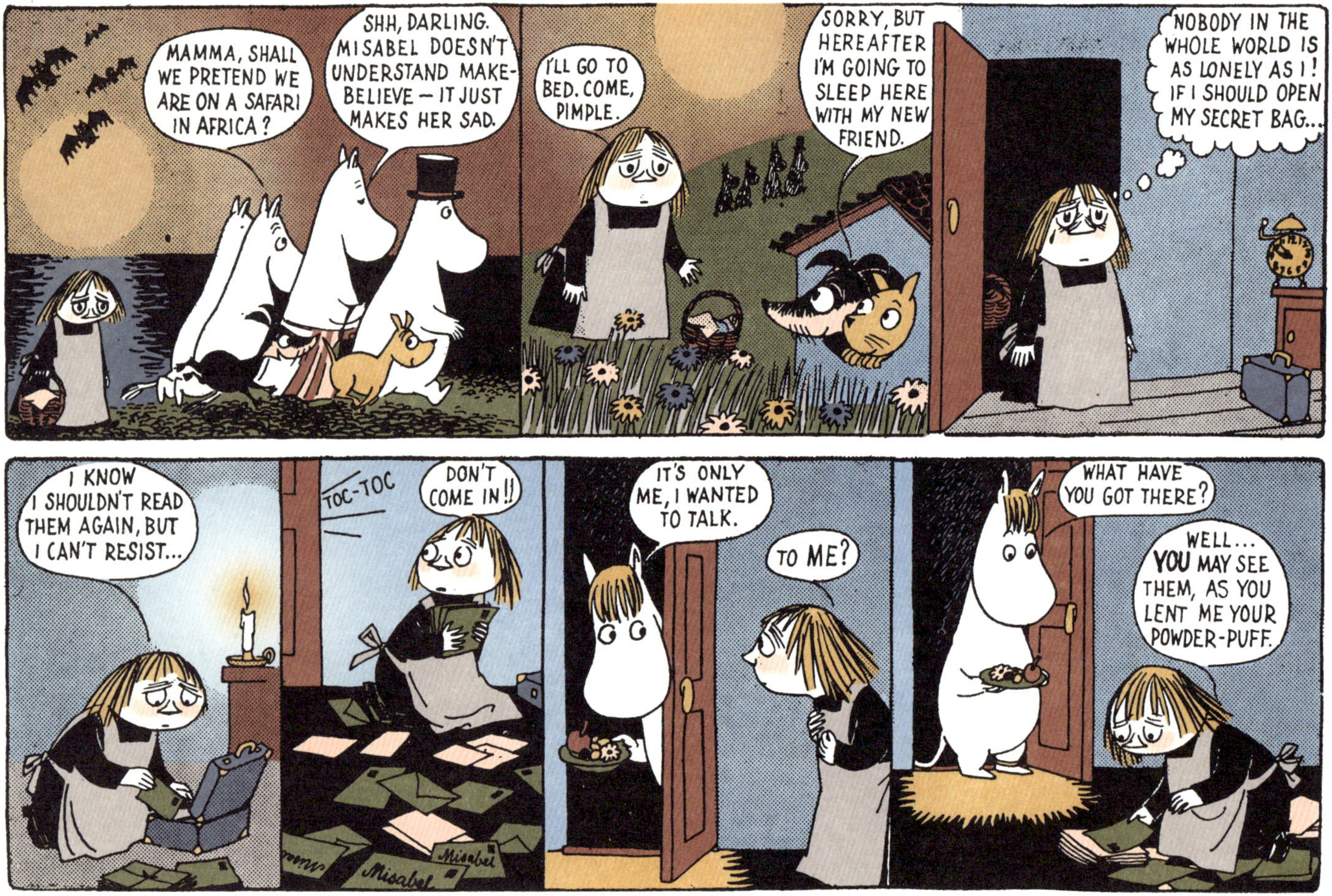
MAMMA, SHALL WE PRETEND WE ARE ON A SAFARI IN AFRICA?
SHH, DARLING. MISABEL DOESN'T UNDERSTAND MAKE-BELIEVE – IT JUST MAKES HER SAD.
I'LL GO TO BED. COME, PIMPLE.
SORRY, BUT HEREAFTER I'M GOING TO SLEEP HERE WITH MY NEW FRIEND.
NOBODY IN THE WHOLE WORLD IS AS LONELY AS I! IF I SHOULD OPEN MY SECRET BAG...
I KNOW I SHOULDN'T READ THEM AGAIN, BUT I CAN'T RESIST...
TOC-TOC
DON'T COME IN!!
Misabel
Misabel
IT'S ONLY ME, I WANTED TO TALK.
TO ME?
WHAT HAVE YOU GOT THERE?
WELL... **YOU** MAY SEE THEM, AS YOU LENT ME YOUR POWDER-PUFF.

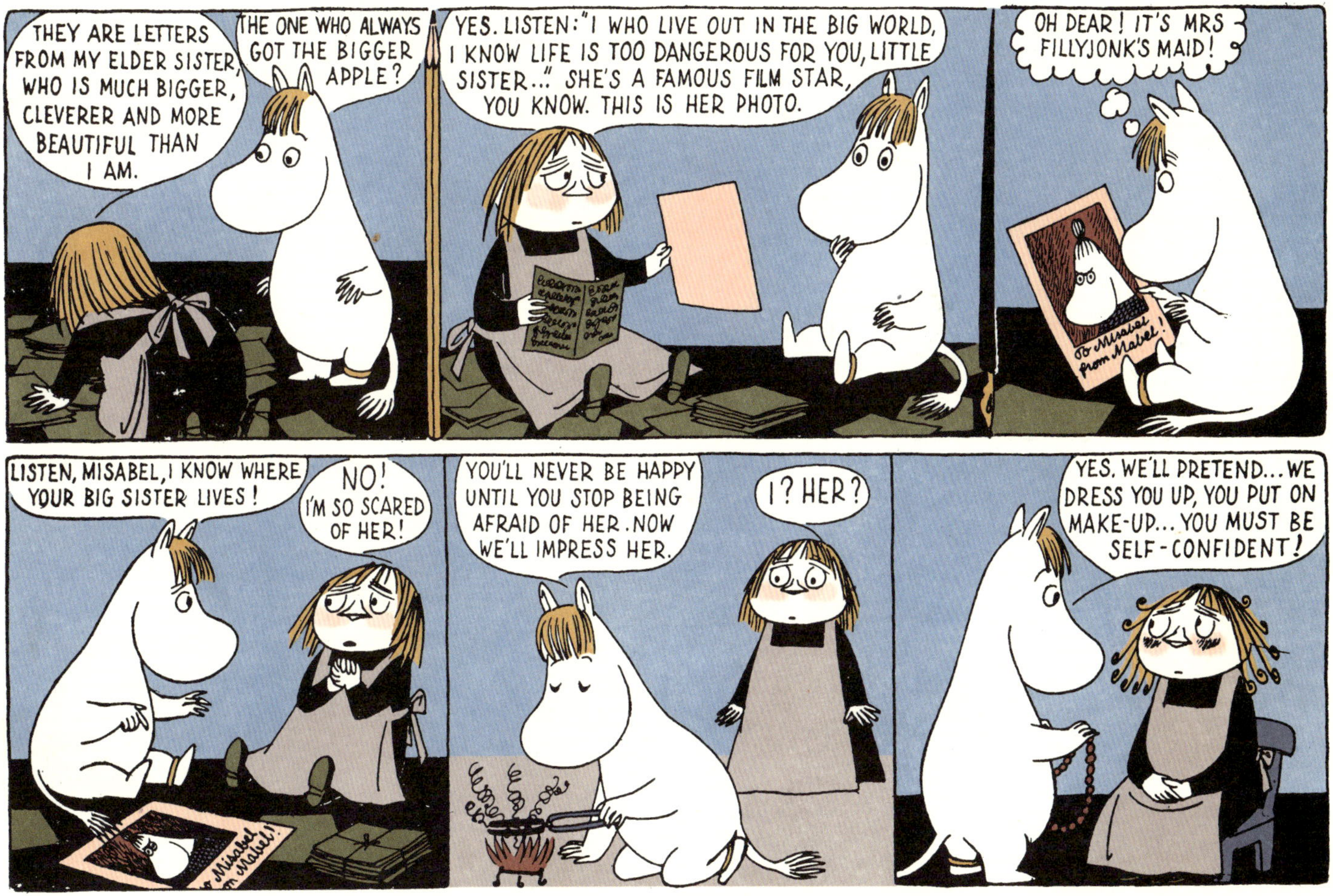
THEY ARE LETTERS FROM MY ELDER SISTER, WHO IS MUCH BIGGER, CLEVERER AND MORE BEAUTIFUL THAN I AM.
THE ONE WHO ALWAYS GOT THE BIGGER APPLE?
YES. LISTEN: "I WHO LIVE OUT IN THE BIG WORLD, I KNOW LIFE IS TOO DANGEROUS FOR YOU, LITTLE SISTER..." SHE'S A FAMOUS FILM STAR, YOU KNOW. THIS IS HER PHOTO.
OH DEAR! IT'S MRS FILLYJONK'S MAID!
To Misabel from Mabel!
LISTEN, MISABEL, I KNOW WHERE YOUR BIG SISTER LIVES!
NO! I'M SO SCARED OF HER!
YOU'LL NEVER BE HAPPY UNTIL YOU STOP BEING AFRAID OF HER. NOW WE'LL IMPRESS HER.
I? HER?
YES. WE'LL PRETEND... WE DRESS YOU UP, YOU PUT ON MAKE-UP... YOU MUST BE SELF-CONFIDENT!

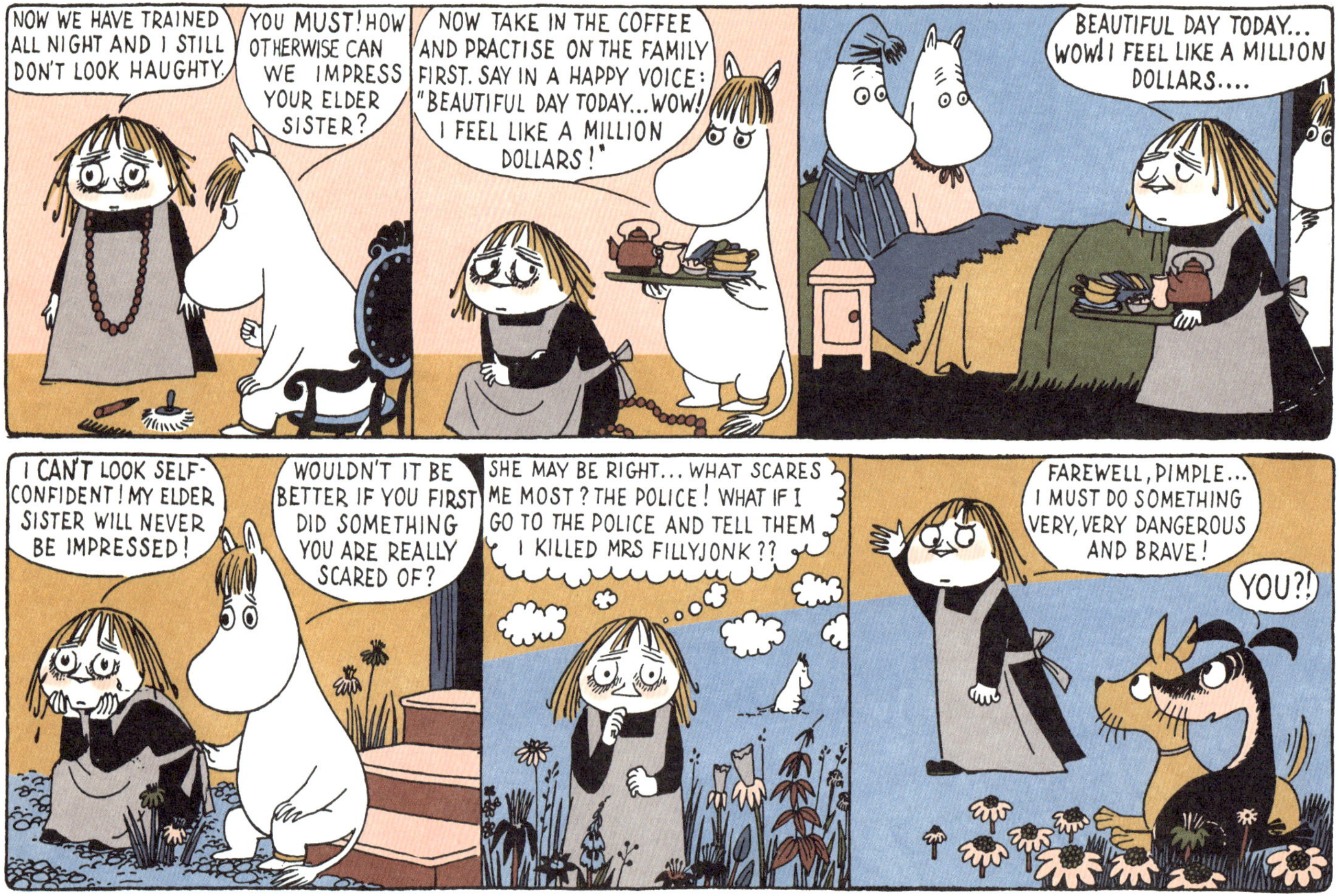
NOW WE HAVE TRAINED ALL NIGHT AND I STILL DON'T LOOK HAUGHTY.
YOU MUST! HOW OTHERWISE CAN WE IMPRESS YOUR ELDER SISTER?
NOW TAKE IN THE COFFEE AND PRACTISE ON THE FAMILY FIRST. SAY IN A HAPPY VOICE: "BEAUTIFUL DAY TODAY... WOW! I FEEL LIKE A MILLION DOLLARS!"
BEAUTIFUL DAY TODAY... WOW! I FEEL LIKE A MILLION DOLLARS....
I CAN'T LOOK SELF-CONFIDENT! MY ELDER SISTER WILL NEVER BE IMPRESSED!
WOULDN'T IT BE BETTER IF YOU FIRST DID SOMETHING YOU ARE REALLY SCARED OF?
SHE MAY BE RIGHT... WHAT SCARES ME MOST? THE POLICE! WHAT IF I GO TO THE POLICE AND TELL THEM I KILLED MRS FILLYJONK??
FAREWELL, PIMPLE... I MUST DO SOMETHING VERY, VERY DANGEROUS AND BRAVE!
YOU?!

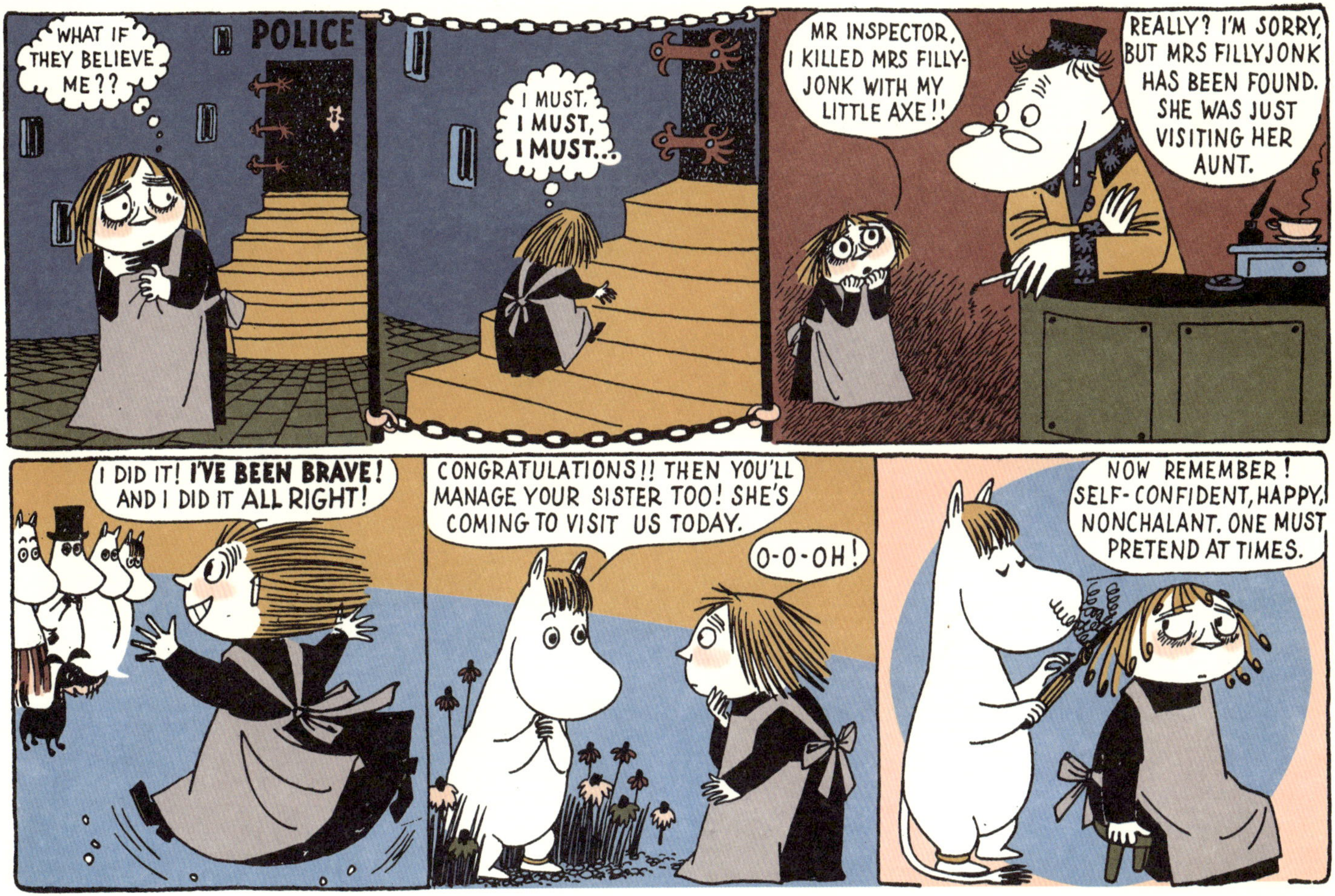

WHAT IF THEY BELIEVE ME??
POLICE
I MUST, I MUST, I MUST...
MR INSPECTOR, I KILLED MRS FILLY-JONK WITH MY LITTLE AXE!!
REALLY? I'M SORRY, BUT MRS FILLYJONK HAS BEEN FOUND. SHE WAS JUST VISITING HER AUNT.
I DID IT! I'VE BEEN BRAVE! AND I DID IT ALL RIGHT!
CONGRATULATIONS!! THEN YOU'LL MANAGE YOUR SISTER TOO! SHE'S COMING TO VISIT US TODAY.
O-O-OH!
NOW REMEMBER! SELF-CONFIDENT, HAPPY, NONCHALANT. ONE MUST PRETEND AT TIMES.

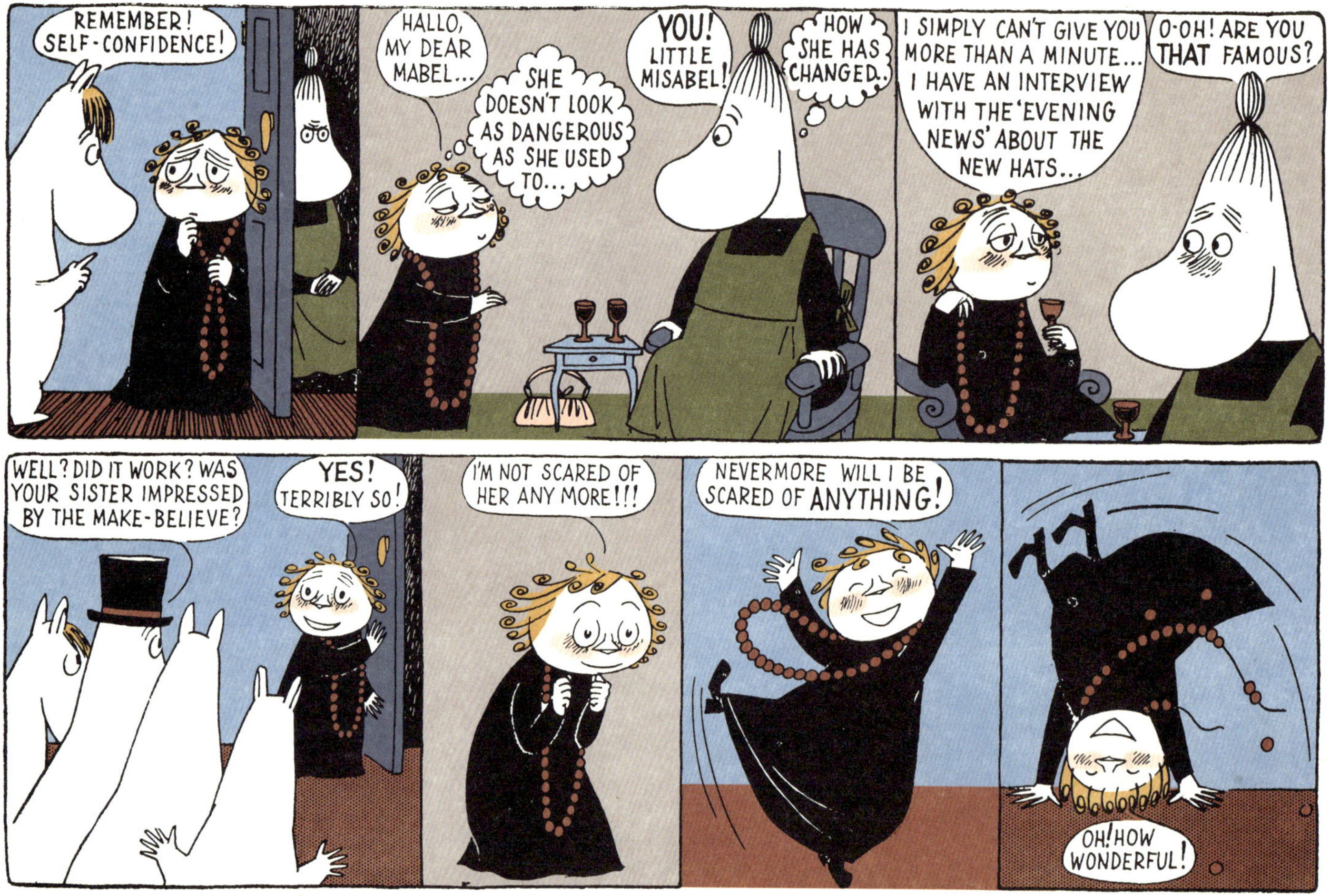
REMEMBER! SELF-CONFIDENCE!
HALLO, MY DEAR MABEL...
SHE DOESN'T LOOK AS DANGEROUS AS SHE USED TO...
YOU! LITTLE MISABEL!
HOW SHE HAS CHANGED..
I SIMPLY CAN'T GIVE YOU MORE THAN A MINUTE... I HAVE AN INTERVIEW WITH THE 'EVENING NEWS' ABOUT THE NEW HATS...
O-OH! ARE YOU THAT FAMOUS?
WELL? DID IT WORK? WAS YOUR SISTER IMPRESSED BY THE MAKE-BELIEVE?
YES! TERRIBLY SO!
I'M NOT SCARED OF HER ANY MORE!!!
NEVERMORE WILL I BE SCARED OF ANYTHING!
OH! HOW WONDERFUL!

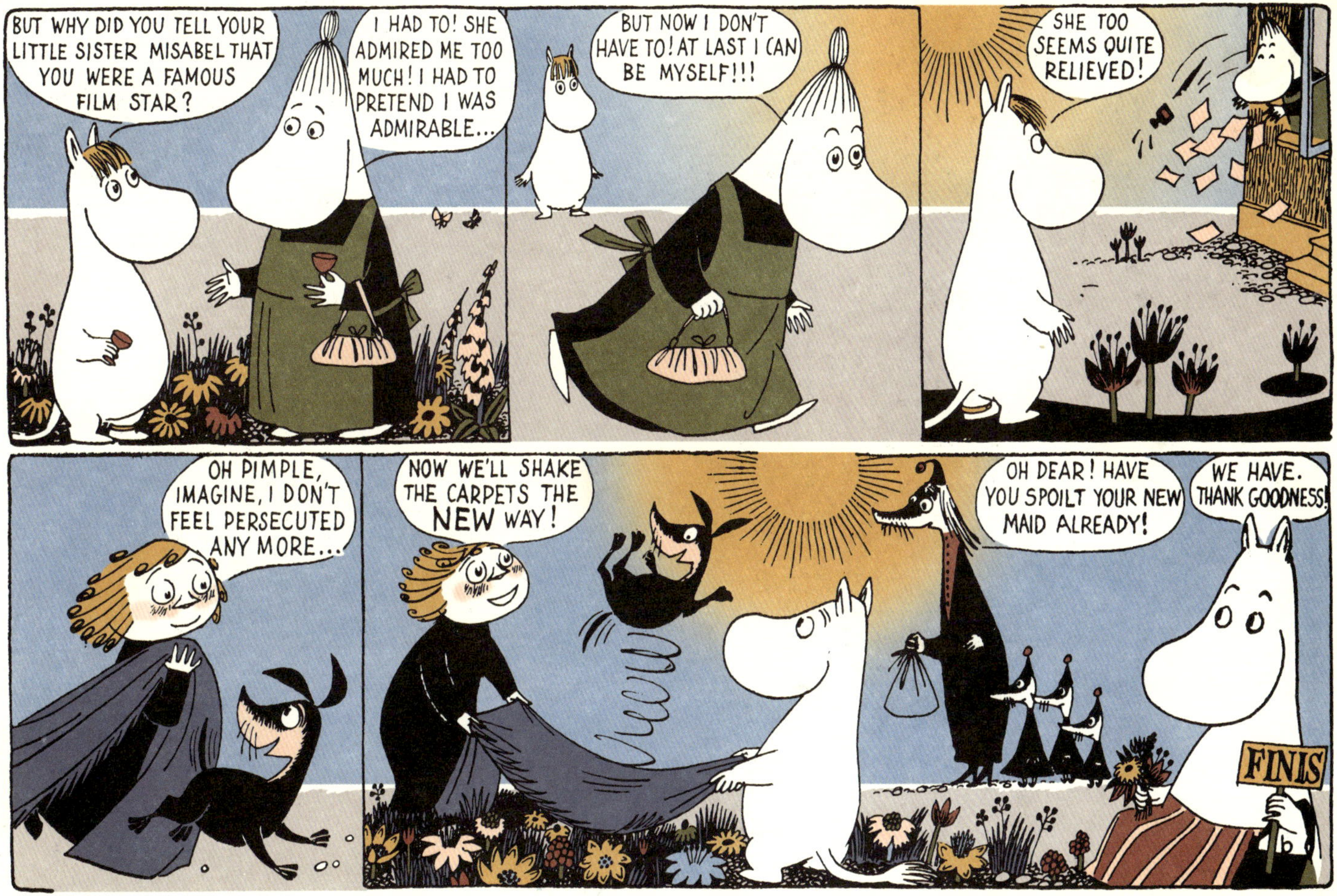

BUT WHY DID YOU TELL YOUR LITTLE SISTER MISABEL THAT YOU WERE A FAMOUS FILM STAR?
I HAD TO! SHE ADMIRED ME TOO MUCH! I HAD TO PRETEND I WAS ADMIRABLE...
BUT NOW I DON'T HAVE TO! AT LAST I CAN BE MYSELF!!!
SHE TOO SEEMS QUITE RELIEVED!
OH PIMPLE, IMAGINE, I DON'T FEEL PERSECUTED ANY MORE...
NOW WE'LL SHAKE THE CARPETS THE NEW WAY!
OH DEAR! HAVE YOU SPOILT YOUR NEW MAID ALREADY!
WE HAVE. THANK GOODNESS!
FINIS

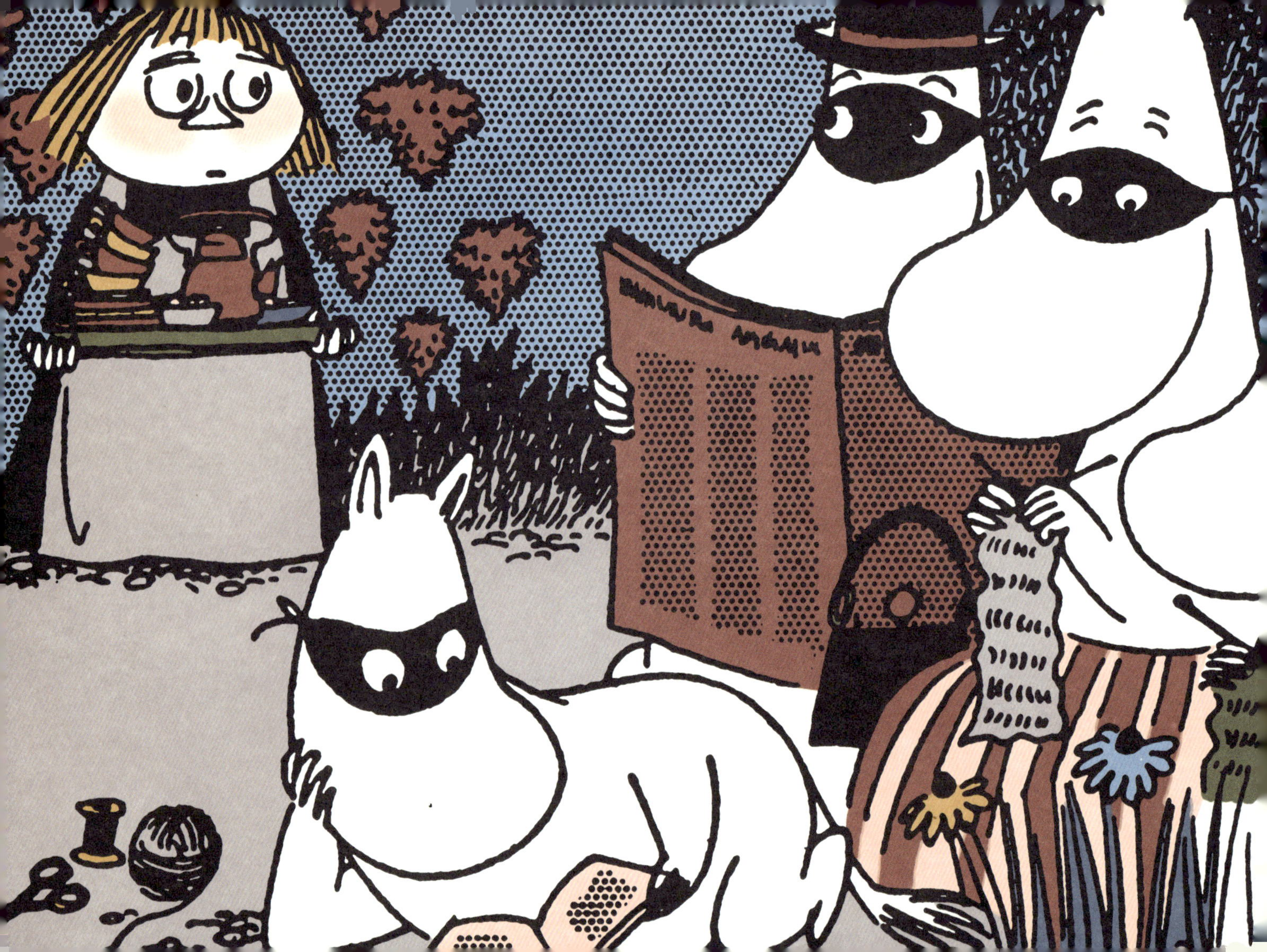

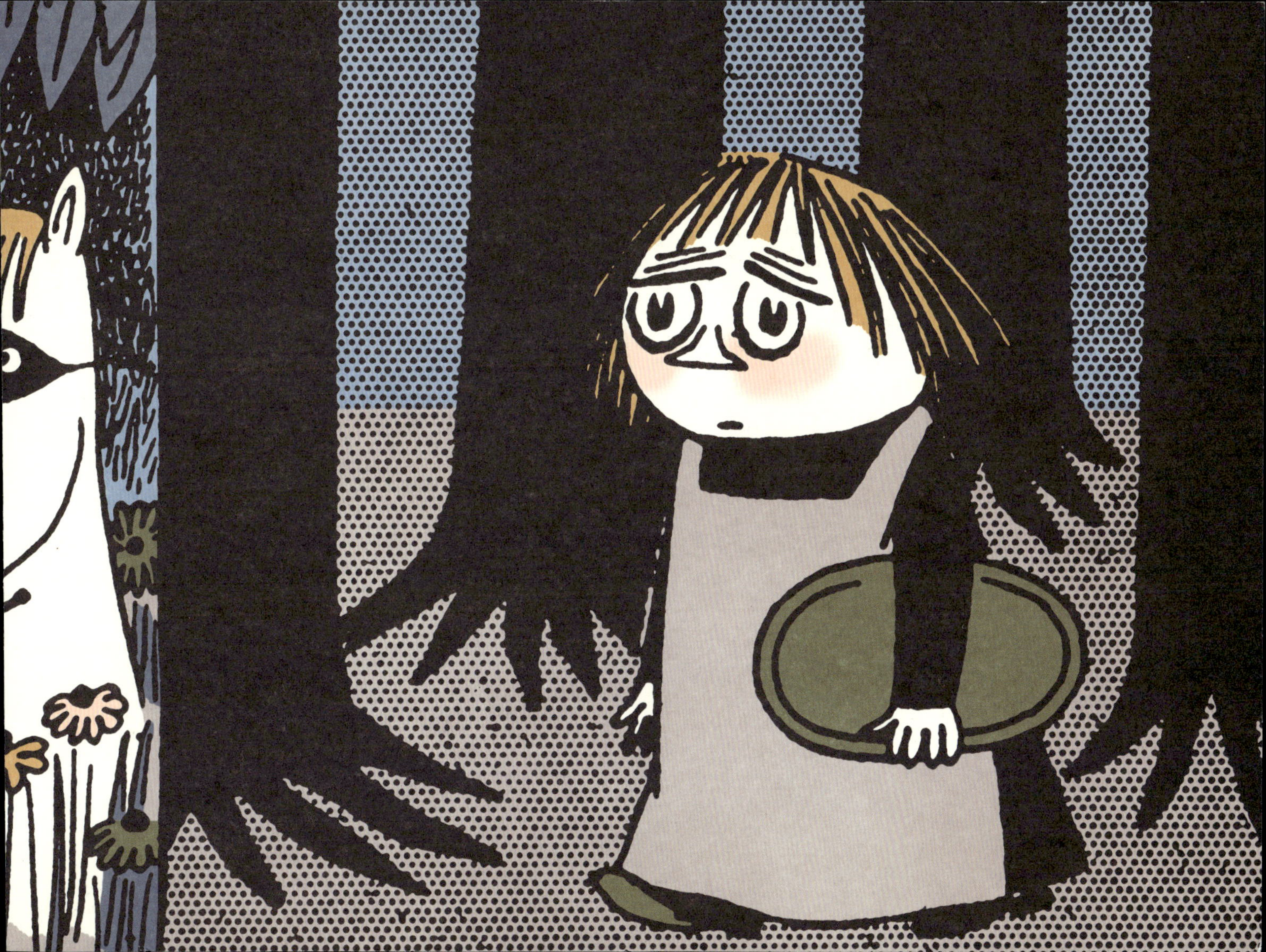

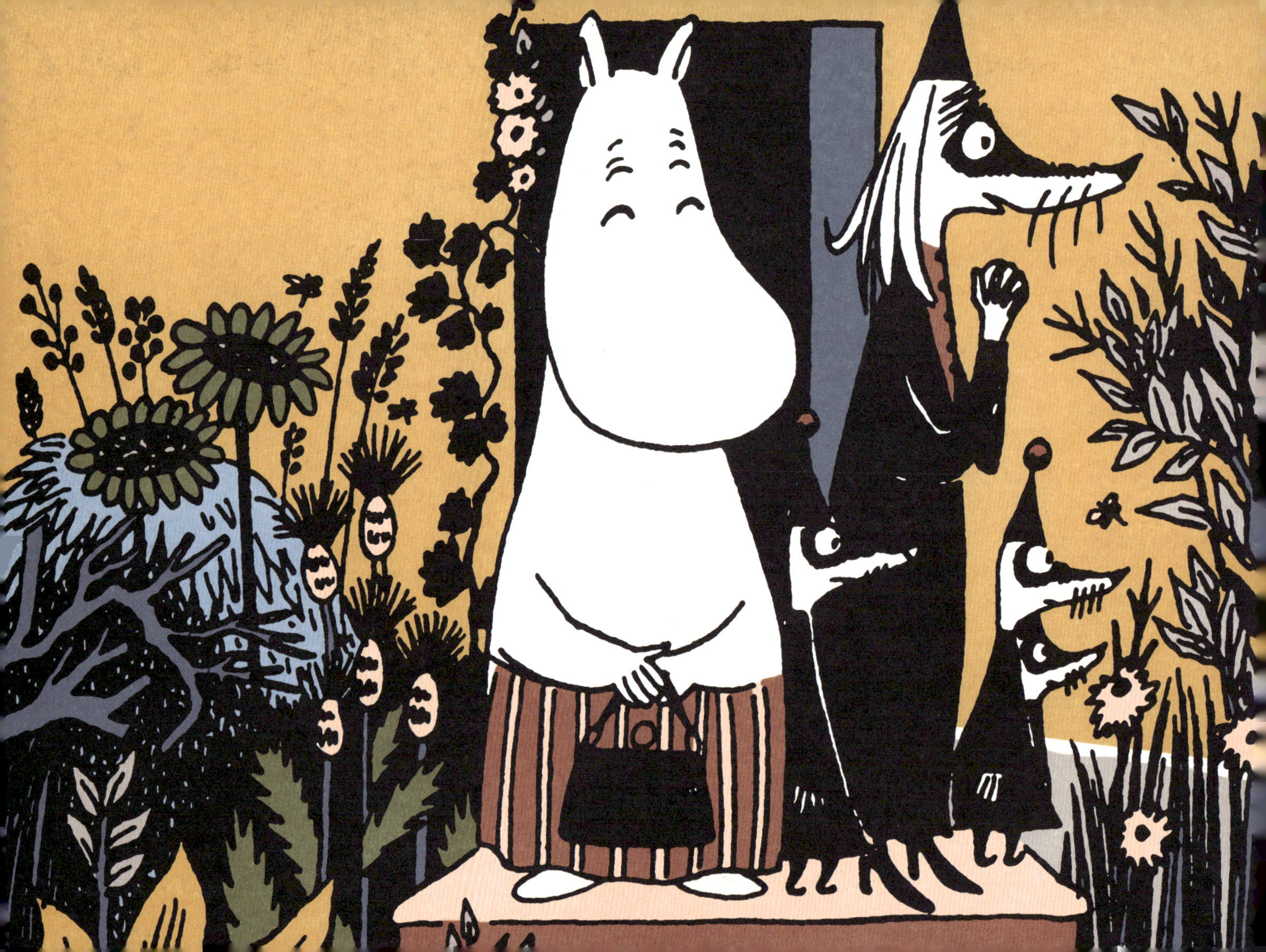

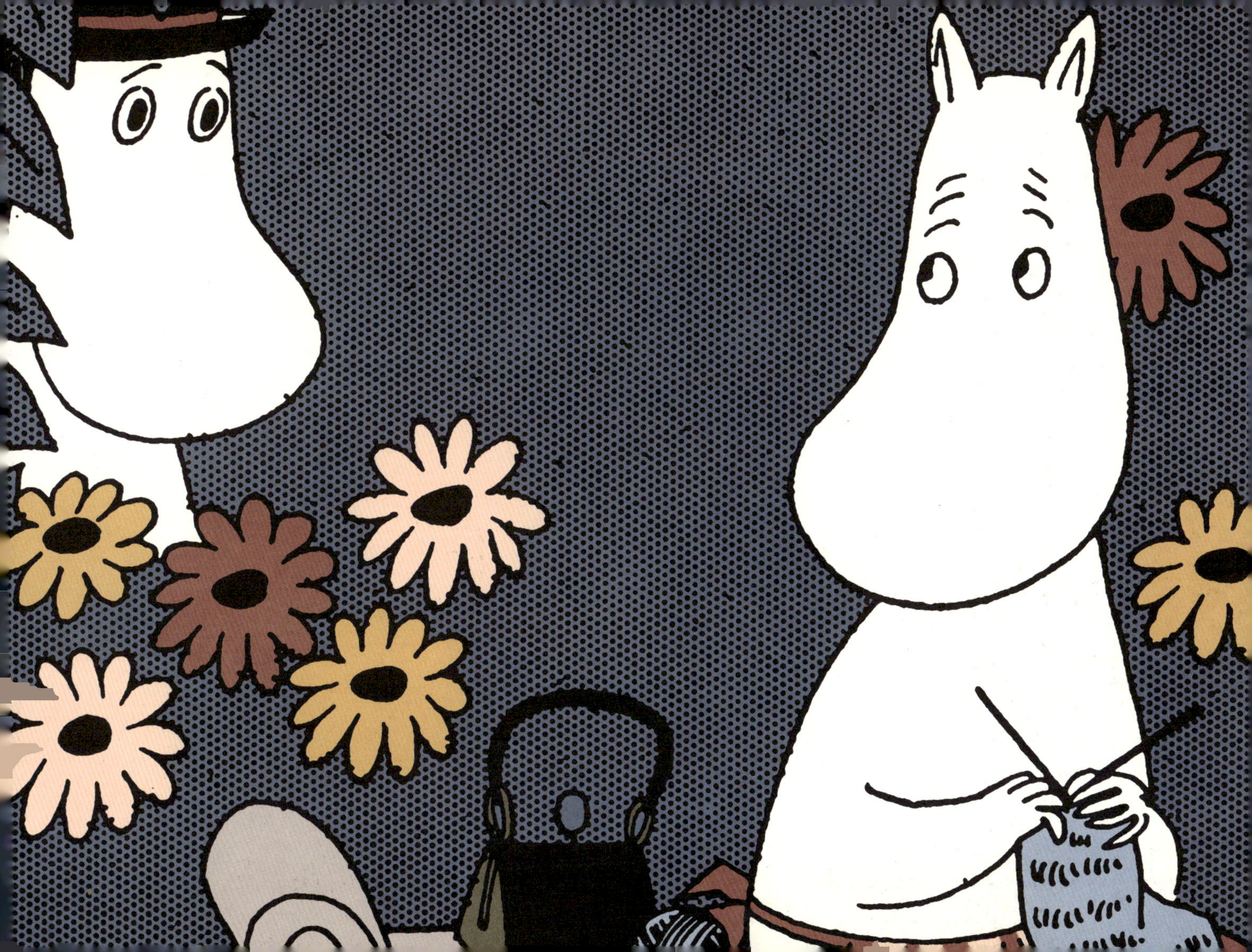

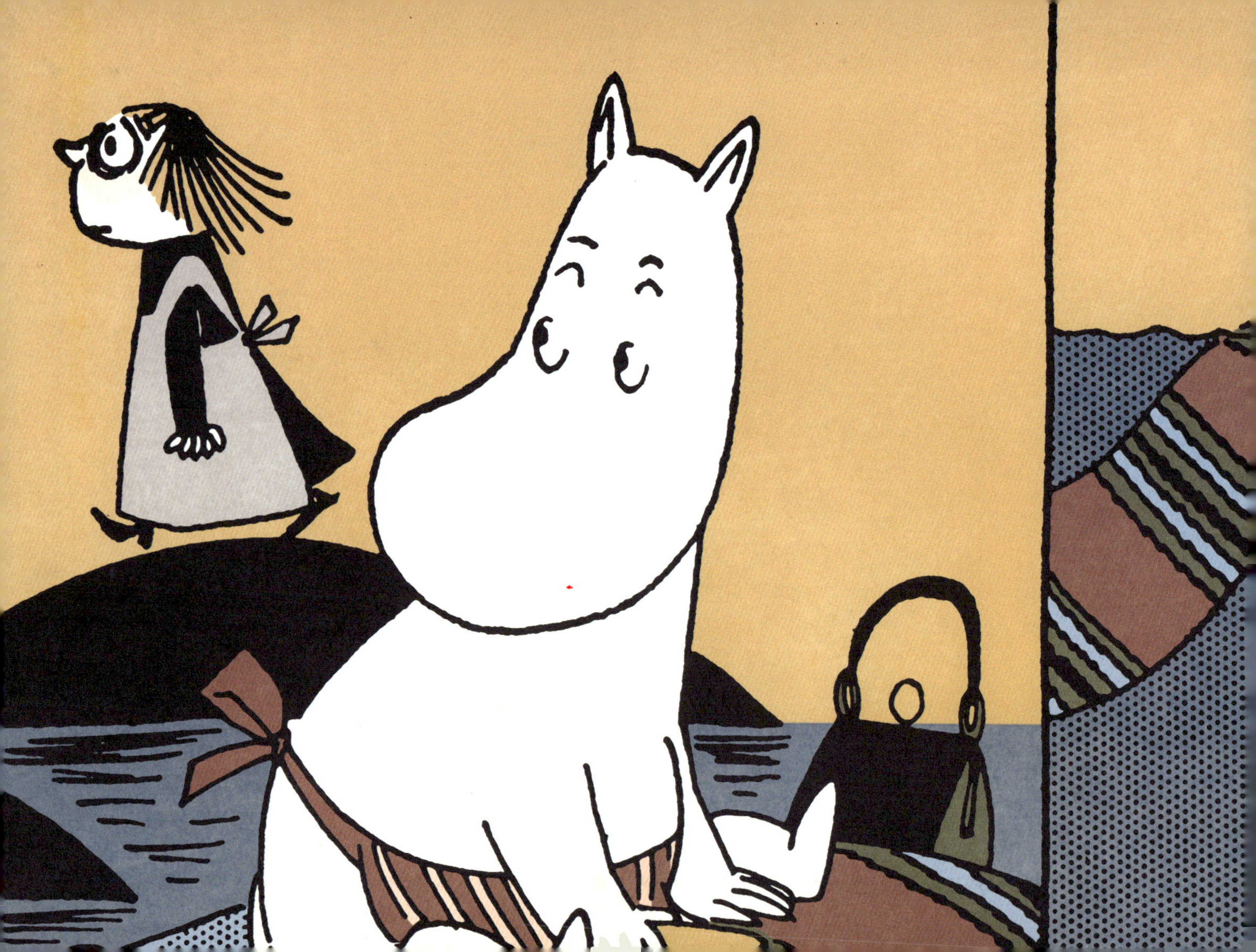